Antiques and Alibis

Wendy H Jones

Donna
So nice to meet you
Wendy H. Jones

ISBN: 978-0-9956457-4-5

DEDICATION

To Michelle Titherington for her inspiration for at least one part of this book.

ACKNOWLEDGMENTS

To all those who have waited so patiently for this book to come out. It has been long in the making.

To all my readers who encourage me to carry on writing. I truly would not be doing this without you.

To Chris Longmuir, fellow crime writer and friend, for everything she does to support me. I appreciate it, Chris. More than you will ever know.

.

1

I'm Cass Claymore, redhead, biker chick, ex ballerina and Private Investigator.

Oh, did I mention the dead body at my feet? The worst part, I'm not sure if I killed him or someone else performed the dirty deed. My days are not usually cluttered up with the recently deceased. So, a difficult call for me.

Aged about thirtyish, clean-shaven, and wearing designer brogues. Not your average lowlife who'd end up dead. Unless the shoes were nicked, of course. The way my week was panning out, I'd probably bumped off some visiting Laird. Might he have died of natural causes? Bending over, I peered at him. He didn't have the look of someone who'd shuffled off this mortal coil voluntarily.

What had I got myself into? A queasy feeling started in the pit of my stomach. Turning away from the corpse I became reacquainted with the hummus sandwich I'd had for my lunch.

I pulled out my phone and pressed the first 9.

2

Two weeks earlier

It's been said that alcohol is the curse of man.

I'll see that and raise you boredom. Boredom wins hands down. How much tidying and rearranging can one woman take? I mean, what's the point of owning a Detective Agency if you've nothing to detect? I stabbed my pencil into the pad. Several times. Did I feel better? Not in the slightest.

I inherited the Claymore Detective Agency from my recently deceased uncle. Unfortunately, I didn't inherit his customers, all of whom deserted to a more testosterone-fuelled environment.

This left me alone, with money dwindling away at the speed of water from a cracked dam. Mostly because the office had been smartened up. Out went the dark panels and in came yellow painted walls and bright prints. It looked lovely. My bank manager thought differently. He had this strange idea I should deposit money in my account. I should be kicking the heck out of bad guys. Instead, I'm sharpening pencils.

I was in the kitchen grinding some Arabica coffee beans. The beans may be considered extravagant given my state of penury. Brewing coffee always manages to convince me otherwise. The early warning creak of the office door sent a frisson of danger zinging along my nerve ends. Goodness knows why as I'd had no enquires for my services so far.

I wiped my hands, on a fuschia pink tea towel, hurled it at the sink, and darted into the office. As I arrived a volcano erupted from behind the desk. A lava burst of fur and bone sprang at the elegant figure standing in my doorway.

"Eagal, no!"

The booming sound of his own barking shattered the walls and rendered the stupid mutt deaf.

"Eagal." I launched myself after him.

The woman went flying. The hound launched a full-frontal attack of tongue and drool. If he had been a fluffy wee terrier there wouldn't have been much of a problem. We're talking Bernese Mountain Dog, standing two feet at the shoulder and weighing a hundred and ten pounds. True to his breed he drooled for Scotland.

I grabbed his collar and yanked it hard. Twice. This resulted in him shaking himself and me executing a flawless pirouette. I charged back into the fray pulling a couple of biscuits from my pocket. The treat had him bouncing in my direction and once more behind the desk.

The woman, a dazed expression on her face, struggled to her feet. A blob of makeup-tinged drool trickled down her face. I watched in horror as it dripped to the floor. "What was..." A moment's pause and the only word she came up with, "...that?"

"So sorry. Are you all right? Let me help."

A general brushing down and straightening of the woman's designer clothes accompanied my words.

I offered her the bathroom and a coffee.

"How safe will it be?"

I assured her total safety on both counts. She headed for the bathroom. I chucked a few treats at the volcano from the stash in my top drawer.

The woman reappeared with makeup reapplied, her hair solid with hairspray. I shook her hand.

"Cass Claymore. Please, sit down."

My potential client perched on two inches of chair and placed her hat on her lap. A Rosie Olivia original, if not mistaken. She examined the ginormous solitaire on her left finger, then her gaze lifted and her deep green eyes stared straight into mine.

"Lady Lucinda Lamont." She rummaged in a bag that could hold Eagal and pulled out a business card. Thick, embossed, and displaying the Lamont family crest. The address showed a family pile situated in the wilds of Aberdeenshire. Lucinda was a long way from home.

She took a sip of her coffee from the bone china mug and held it in her mouth for several seconds before swallowing. "I see you know your coffee."

I wished she'd tell me about the blasted job. I was patient up to a point; this job required it. She tested my temper to its narrow limits. I kept shtum. Uncle Will taught me this netted the most information. I reflected beating people might work better.

"My son's favourite teddy bear has gone missing."

A teddy. All this hurry up and wait and my job entailed finding a cuddly toy. Seriously. Mike Hammer would turn in his grave.

I must work on doing the enigmatic thing with my face. Lady Lucy responded, "It may be humdrum, but not to Theo. It's his favourite toy. Inconsolable doesn't cover it. My nerves can't take much more. Name your price."

A few rapid mental calculations and I worked out how much I needed to stay solvent for a few months. I added a few quid on for good measure.

"Five thousand pounds up front, fifty-five pounds an hour. Seventy at night. Plus VAT."
Way over the going limit around these parts. Especially for someone who hadn't even finished their diploma. And I wasn't remotely VATable.

"Done."

I reined in my astonishment and drew out a contract, quickly filling the blanks. She signed with an Onoto fountain pen and purple ink. This dame had style. She made out a cheque for five thousand smackeroonies and I had my first client.

After some rather dumb but necessary questioning, I discovered the teddy was vintage Steiff, still with button in ear. With tan fur. His name, Bartholomew, Bart for short, and also a family heirloom. She handed me a photo of a blonde-haired cherub clutching said teddy. I was in business.

"If you don't mind me asking, why did you choose this agency?"
I just couldn't help myself. Aberdeen's chock-full of hotshot investigators and I didn't have any reputation to speak of.

"You came highly recommended from one of my husband's friends, David Stallins."

Desperate Dave! I went to school with him and he was a weasel. Time had chiselled the weasel look more deeply. Why did he recommend me?

Lucinda placed her hat at the correct angle. "If you want more clients you might want to leave the monster at home."

I saw her point. Eagal is Gaelic for terror. The mutt took on the mantle with vigour and ran with it at every opportunity. The last time I left him in my flat he managed to take three doors off their hinges and eat a whole chocolate cake. This gave him the runs and I had to burn the living room carpet. I rather liked the thought of returning to my home and finding it in one piece, but the dog came as a package with the business.

My father threatened to shoot me if I got rid of his late brother's faithful companion. I knew what his aim was like and wasn't taking any chances.

So, began the case of the travelling teddy.

3

As Lady Lucy walked out the door I performed a wee celebratory dance. An elegant double pirouette and a devéloppé reminded me why I had given up my passion. Pain, quick and severe, halted me. I limped over to a chair and rubbed my knee. Eagal joined the dance. His balletic abilities consisted of standing on pointes and slobbering. Extricating myself I headed in the direction of a washcloth.

Once dribble free I threw myself into my seat ready for a concentrated few hours detecting. Arranged in a thinking pose, the first flaw in my plan made itself apparent. I had no clue where I should start. Dear departed Uncle Will believed someone on crutches shouldn't be detecting. My time before his demise I spent answering the phone and doing the odd bit of filing. My days since, taken up with decorating. And buying new stationery.

I pulled a heavy tome off my shelf - Private Investigators Handbook: Scotland. A satisfying thunk shook the scarred oak desk. A remnant of the great cleanup, it reminded me of Uncle Will. A yellow legal pad and pristine file joined it. Arranging these made me feel professional. The book open, I thumbed to the chapter on starting a case.

I chucked a bone at the dog mountain to keep him occupied. He crunched, and I worked, for a couple of hours. The legal pad filled up with copious notes of the 'perhaps try' variety.

Eagal leaping up and the harsh squeal of the office door broke my concentration. My best friend, Lexi, catapulted through the door and spread-eagled herself against the wall. No mean feat for someone six-foot-tall and weighing as much as a pregnant highland cow.

"Cass Claymore, when will you do something about that canine health and safety hazard." She used all her power to shove Eagal's face away from hers. He managed to perform one more all-encompassing lick. Never one to shy away from his duties, he made sure any passing human got scrubbed clean.

I kicked the remains of the bone against the skirting. This had him bounding back, all thoughts of Lexi flown from his head. Not only is he badly behaved, he's also the thickest hound since time began.

"Sorry, Lex. Short of a tranquiliser gun, I'm not sure what to do. I'm spending all my hard-earned cash on treats. Talking of cash…"

I announced the news of the case to her.

Her eyes lit up at my mention of how much hard cash I had to deposit in my bank account. Her face said, 'great stuff'. Her words screamed ulterior motive.

"Excellent. You'll need an assistant then, darling. That's worked out just perfectly."

An unexpected visit from Lexi usually meant my life would change in some major way and not for the better. I loved Lex dearly. Twenty-three years' friendship does that. But she always managed to coerce me into doing something I objected to.

"Assistant? Hang on, Lex. I didn't say anything—"

"I've got just the person. Quill possesses every skill

required of a PI."

This did not bode well. Lexi's chosen profession is a Community Justice Support Worker. The fancy moniker is what used to be called a Criminal Justice Officer. She specialises in finding ex-cons jobs. One was about to be palmed off on me.

"No. Absolutely not. I've barely enough work for *me*."

"All settled then. He'll be here in the morning. Ciao, darling."

"Lex, how can you translate no to yes?"

She blew me a kiss, darted out the door and dashed down the stairs. Her footsteps were astonishingly quiet for one so large.

"What in the name of heavens am I going to do with an assistant?"

Eagal sat up, gave one booming wuff, and settled down again.

His look said, "More people to play with."

My look said I needed to improve at refusing. I barely knew what to do with myself never mind an employee with a 'past'.

4

Bertie Pinkerton, descendant of Alan Pinkerton the original PI, advises in his excellent book that an investigator needs to think outside the box. I didn't even have a box. Also, thinking appeared to be beyond my intelligence level. I had the last known whereabouts of Bart the missing teddy; Duthie Park in Aberdeen. A quick search informed me this covered 44 acres. A cinch then. I rapidly reevaluated my need of an aide.

My requirement to head out correlated with my need of a dog sitter. My firefighter boyfriend was busy putting out fires, so useless as a substitute nanny. I picked up the phone and dialled my granddad. Eighty-five years old, he appeared sixty and acted twenty. He had a way with the mutt. It rolled over like a wee sook at one word from Elgin Claymore. Mhairi, my granny, frequently stated it was about the only thing the stupid moron was suitable for. She wasn't talking about the dog.

He arrived within the hour. He sported jeans, a stripy blazer and a boater hat a la Dick Van Dyke in Mary Poppins.

"The car's yours if you want to borrow it, hen."

"Thanks, but I'll take the bike."

"Your mum's no' going to be happy."

"Let's keep it our little secret. Can you take Eagal back to her's if I'm not back by knocking off time? Your duties until then include manning the phone and taking messages."

He agreed. I've had him wrapped around my little

finger since my first toothless smile. I kissed his rough cheek and headed in the direction of my motorbike.

An unusual choice of transport for an ex ballet dancer? You bet. Focus on the word *ex*. My love affair with motorbikes started when I remember seeing my first one whizz past at age two. My dancing career meant the love affair went nowhere. Doomed before it started. My first response when the doctor proclaimed my *ex* status; purchase a black Yamaha XV950R. A sporty little number, light enough for someone with a knee injury, yet powerful and handles well in all road conditions. It gives me the freedom only a Pas de Deux Grand, at the Royal Opera House previously brought. The same thrill coursed through my body and brought me alive.

The bike was kept in a garage so secure the police might enquire what I hid in there. Necessary against low lives, weather and the prying eyes of my mother.

I adopted the leather-clad, biker chick look, hopped on the bike and used the remote to open and close the garage door. My knee injury had been the result of an altercation with a drunk driver. I utilised the compensation money well, the bike and the garage being two of the first things on which I splashed the cash. Those and my flat. The flat is an entirely different kettle of boiling renovations altogether.

Some lateral thinking convinced me I needed to chuck normal clothes in my panniers. It seemed to me any self-respecting PI should be adaptable. More to the point, my parents' house featured later in the day.

The revamp of the city centre meant it resembled a car park more than a road system. The bike meant I dodged the traffic and soon settled into a steady rhythm on the A90 to Aberdeen. Quiet for a main artery, so little concentration involved. This gave me time to think and stash a few ideas for plans B, C and D. My confidence in the robustness of plan A did not overwhelm.

5

In Aberdeen, the next little flaw in my plan became speedily apparent. A fast acreage stretched out in front of me. I snagged a free map of the park from the visitors' centre, grabbed an overpriced coffee from the café and plonked myself on a nearby chair. Opening the map, I pulled out a pen and circled several likely dropping points. The enchantment of a child, and the stamina of a young au pair, guided my choice. The pen drew a pleasingly tight little meandering circle.

The child's play park leapt out immediately. Maybe a little obvious?

Flaw number three hit me like a boxer on speed when I tipped up at said humongous play park. I should have brought one of my numerous nephews and nieces with me. A leather-clad woman with bright ginger hair didn't blend in. Not with a bunch of screaming toddlers, designer-clad yummy mummies and Swiss au pairs. I got some odd stares and a few hands hovered over iPhones. The 999 thoughts, fluttering at the outskirts of their brains, were apparent at a million paces.

I left them to it and hoofed it back to the bike. Taking off my jacket I stuffed it in the panniers. Rummaging around in the pannier netted a coral pink lipstick which I applied liberally. Then tied up my hair. This might make me appear more human being and less a demented stalker. Or, worse case scenario, a paedophile.

Adopting a confident air, I returned to the playground and strode up to a mother dressed head to toe in Gucci. Odd sort of clothing choice for a day at the park, but then again, who made me the guru.

"My little one's lost her teddy. Any chance you've seen one?" I shoved a photo in her face while using the poshest voice I could muster. I had high hopes of blending in.

A shake of her head sent the woman's ruby drop earrings jangling. She turned back to observing little Harry stuff sand in his mouth.

I shivered at the thought of what might be in there. Sand can hide a whole heap of revolting garbage.

Rinsed and repeated several times, the question grew old. Until one frazzled father said, "That's vintage Steiff. Try the auctions and shove off."

He raised a worthy point. The teddy would be long gone. Still, I was here, on a bonnie day, and my optimistic streak kicked in. My brand-new leathers took somewhat of a beating as I crawled about under bushes. Toddlers get everywhere so best to check some of the less obvious places. Not a teddy to be found.

I found out many other things about the underside of bushes whilst on my foray. Mainly that they tear at your clothes. And your arms. I'm no soothsayer, but I foretold an appointment with antiseptic cream in my future. Also, they are a receptacle for the darker things in life, like condoms and used needles. A rat eyeballed me as it scurried past. Being the youngest of eight kids, five of them brothers, had its advantages. A positive menagerie of pets, including rats and snakes, knocked the squeamish right out of the court at an early age. Alexander, the owner of most of the animals, is now a qualified vet. Comes in useful to keep Eagal's vet bills down. Given his attraction to trouble, he has a lot of these. We've struck a deal of the 'I'm his little sister so he does it all for nothing' kind.

I crawled out from under the bush and brushed off the detritus of an investigator's life; then applied a wet wipe to my hands. They're a required addition to an investigators toolkit. A female PI, anyway. Tickling the ivories is a pastime of mine. I needed my long slender fingers to stay in reasonable nick. The PI's in books have it much easier as they just follow their marks around and sit in smoky bars drinking Dark and Stormies. After a minute's thought, I wiped my leathers with the wet wipe. Crumpled suits might be de rigueur for PI's, but not in this one's world.

One other thing I discovered about the underside of bushes is that they stink of wet earth and middens. I now wore the scent as a perfume, limiting further questioning. Wet hobo is not a cologne which endears one to people.

The thought of Dark and Stormies had me longing for a crisp Château de Berne Provence Rosé. Straight from the fridge, it would slip down nicely. Instead, I posted several notices with Bart's picture and my mobile number. I ramped up the pathos for effect:

Lost
One Teddy Bear
Much-loved toy
Child inconsolable
Reward for safe return

What the reward would be eluded me. The five

thousand squids were mentally spent. On office rent, food and the bottle of wine. At £11 a bottle some consider it a luxury. I consider it an essential food item. Given my original career, I tend to eat healthily. Ballet dancers must be stick thin. This is even more important if you're the principal dancer, being held aloft by a proportionately skinny male equivalent. Fine wine is my one exception. Any self-respecting PI should have a vice. Pinkerton would approve.

6

I proceeded in a southerly direction, the panther-like purr of the bike lulling me into a false sense of security. This meant the blue flashing lights took me by surprise. I pulled over. Not out of any sense of being a law-abiding citizen. More because my mother would not take kindly to a criminal in the family.

The door of the police car opened. Out stepped a long streak of bacon and a green-eyed imp. Bacon's face was decorated with sunspecs and an unimpressed look. He appeared to be about ten. The imp had assumed the persona of the Cheshire Cat in full grin mode.

I pulled off my helmet and my long ginger hair dropped straight down my back, reminding me of the ambient temperature. I watched them approach wondering how this would play out.

"Are you aware you jumped a red light?" God changed the breed when he made Bacon. "We would like you to accompany us down the station."

"We can't arrest her," hissed the imp. "She's Clay's sister. Plus, she's some sort of celebrity around these parts."

"She's a chick who was speeding."

"Call me a chick again and I'll give you something real to arrest me for."

I wondered if decking him might be an option. Maybe not. But my Scottish Russian temperament was willing to take a risk.

"You'll be called worse than that in the cell down in

my nick. I'm adding threatening a police officer to your long list of offences."

"Oi, hothead, no one's being chucked in a cell."

The imp was Alice, my brother's best friend. She handed the young officer a ten-pound note. Paying him off? Bit of a cheapskate if you ask me. I'm worth more than a tenner.

"Go buy yourself an ice cream and cool down. Life's too short to be arresting Claymores. They'll all gang up and Dundee's awash with them."

"I'll be reporting this."

"Go for it son. I'm sure Clay will be keen to discuss it with you."

Clay was my older brother, Lachlan. Currently gainfully employed as a Sergeant in CID or whatever they were called since the changeover to Police Scotland. He'd been fighting my battles since the minute I shot out of the womb and took my first argumentative gasp. Sorting out any mess I got myself into came as natural as breathing to him.

She made a valid point regarding the glut of Claymores. My grandfather was one of nine. My father one of eleven. My mother's family also did a nice line in breeding large families. Another similar, yet different, seething mass of Petrovs.

Bacon lifted his sunglasses, eyed me up, closed the notebook and shoved it back in a pocket. Disaster averted.

"You need to slow down in future."

"Of course, officer."

As they walked away I heard Bacon say, "I'll be taking this up with Clay."

"Best of luck with that," said the ever-pragmatic

Alice.

Bacon faced an interesting evening. I needed to plan a retreat; miles from my brother. Brotherly love only took me so far.

7

I made it to my parent's house at a more sedate pace and without further mishap. The strong aroma of something exquisite slammed into me the minute I opened the scarred front door. Generations of exuberant Claymores had left their mark on it.

Eagal was nowhere to be seen. My brother, Findlay's, presence on the tartan plaid sofa, told me the mutt was undoubtedly in the garden with his brood. Findlay married the delightful Annie. A midwife, she worked long shifts. Probably to catch a break from Findlay and her offspring. My brother brought his four hyperactive boys over the minute she set foot out the door. His maxim, there is safety in numbers. I waved a cheery hand at him and headed for the kitchen. He waved one weary finger in response. His boys left everyone exhausted.

My mother was hard at work making Khartcho (beef soup with walnuts, to you poor saps lacking Russian parentage) which explained the tantalising aroma. Somewhat unexplainable was the fact she stood by the Aga wearing nothing but matching electric blue bra and pants.
"Your choice of clothing is a bit extreme, Mamah." Despite the fact, Anastasia, my mother, hailed from Glasgow, we still use the Russian derivative of mum. Claymores are not only brave - they like to be different. Although the choice of electric blue for underwear was unusual even for Mamah.

"You try cooking in the throes of menopause. You'll soon find out I'm overdressed for the occasion."

She pushed her hair back from her brow using her arm. Black, in a family of redheads, and also wild. Naturally curly, the heat took it to unheard of heights of frizziness.

"Smells yummy. I'll have salad though."

"Cassandra Claymore, you'll eat the same as everyone else."

"But—"

"My sweat went into the making of a vegetarian version. No more arguments."

"Do what your mother tells you, Cass." My long-suffering father had joined us. He let us kids away with murder, unlike my mother. Her word was law. Even he followed it.

Things were going so well until Lachie arrived.

"Cass Claymore, I was hoping you'd be here."

"I wasn't going that fast."

Regret hit the minute I said it. My carefully laid plans of changing from leathers to shorts were for nowt.

"Cassandra Claymore!"

My Sunday name twice in less than five minutes. Never a favourable sign. Both my mother and Lachie spoke at once. My nieces and nephews joined in chanting my name over and over. Little Sophia provided the percussion section by banging her Tommee Tippee bottle on the table of her antique high chair. She dribbled as accompaniment. My general bollocking got lost in the overall rumpus.

By the time the noise died down, everyone had forgotten what had started it.

I hoped Lachie had also forgotten. His cool stare informed me otherwise. Damn and blast.

A quick overview of my case diffused the situation.

"Not quite up there with chasing after assassins, is it?"

This from Angus, who thinks rising before midday is an adventure. Another of my brothers, he should have been called Peter, the boy who never grew up.

"And just what have you achieved today? Got dressed, did you? True superhero stuff."

"Don't argue with your brother."

My mother emphasised the point by waving a serving spoon around. We all ignored the spray and simply wiped any low-flying sauce from our faces and bodies. Anastasia had a habit of decorating us.

"Have you thought about asking in the junk shops? Someone might have handed it in."

My thoughts ran to, someone would have nicked it. My mother is the eternal optimist.

"It's worth a mint. Tomorrow I'll be trailing around antique shops."

"Leave it to the police, Cass."

Lachlan was even more optimistic than my mother.

"Not a chance. As if you lot are going to be searching for an auld teddy. Besides this is a paying gig."

"You're right. Knock yourself out. That bear's long gone. You might as well make a couple of bob in your fruitless chase."

Eagal interrupted the pleasant exchange by insisting he needed his tea. This was a bit steep considering he'd been chowing down with the best of them since he arrived.

I begged a lift home from my grandfather and went to feed the garbage tip on legs. The wee chancer considered the food he'd received to be a mere snack. A taster for the main event.

A glass of rosé, from the bottle chilling in my fridge, also called my name.

8

By the time I'd spruced up the office and bought my two-wheeled transport and a flat, the readies had run out. Therefore, my humongous home had the aura of a derelict building site. Heavy on the derelict. The one exception being the largest room in the place. This had metamorphosed into a ballet studio complete with top of the range fully sprung flooring. Margot Fonteyn would have been proud.

My morning routine did not vary. It started with an hour's ballet and ended with wholemeal toast and a vegetable shake. Old habits die hard. Halfway through my sweet kale shake an apparition interrupted me in my kitchen. This particular apparition happened to be my boyfriend and he should not have been there. The fact he wore nothing but his pyjama bottoms added to the drama.

Larbert had a suntan to die for and a smile that did something to a woman's insides. My insides that is. His insides were pure ember and could be fanned into flame at the slightest provocation. As Eagal hurtled towards the man his muscles flexed. When the mutt landed square on his chest he didn't move a millimetre. A long tongue swept his face.

"Eagal, down."

The mutt obeyed and sat gazing at his hero while sweeping the floor with his tail.

How come that little technique evades me? Life can be so unfair. I took one last swallow of my shake and chucked the glass in the sink. It settled with a clang next to all the other dishes. PI's have far more important things to do than washing up.

Let me put the pyjama bottoms into context. Larbert lives in the flat upstairs. He is a fireman by profession and knows a million different ways to enter my flat without using a key. None of them so far had involved an axe. Not that I ruled it out. Nothing would surprise me with Larbert involved.

"What are you doing here? It's too early for house calls."

"Shove a couple of slices of toast in for me, sweetheart."

His smile could melt iron, but I remained resolute. Us Claymores didn't give in easily.

"Go toast your own bread. Shove it on a skewer and take it to your next shout."

His response was to grab me and kiss me thoroughly on my traitorous lips. My head said shove off, my heart bring it on. My lips were begging for more, before making an informed decision.

All resolution flew out the window. Dazed I shoved a couple of slices of wholemeal in the toaster.

"Honey?"

"Perfect, sweets."

A pretty stupid question given there was nothing other than honey as decoration for toast. Larbert tended to tip me in the direction of stupidity.

"Bye, sweetheart." He grabbed his toast and disappeared upstairs. A cupboard love type of morning.

Eagal and I walked to work as usual. A straight route down the Perth Road, it takes about twenty minutes. However, Eagal has his own ideas as to the appropriate route to work. It varies according to the vagaries of his pea-sized brain. This means he walks me there rather than the other way around. Today he fancied a jaunt down to Riverside. Not too bad as detours go. I arrived only marginally late. This mattered not one jot as no queue snaked down the street.

Eagal settled behind the desk. The coffee machine called me. I returned to the mutt standing by the door. A stealth attack had been mounted on some poor unsuspecting customer. Or had he? There didn't appear to be a customer or anything else around. The mutt had reached new heights of dumbness. Then I saw a small hand waving from under the fur mountain.

Grief. The dope was smothering a child.

"Eagal." I simultaneously yanked and waved a treat under his nose. This had the desired effect and he leapt back and skittered over the floor. A large thump shook the room as he caromed off the wall. He shook himself, causing a tsunami of air. Somewhat cooling to be truthful.

A man lay on the floor. A rather dapper one, with a well-trimmed beard and standing about four feet tall. Or he would have been if not decorating my lavish parquet flooring.

"Sir, I'm so sorry."

I helped him upright. This proved more difficult than first envisaged. What a weight for one so small.

He tugged on his multicoloured waistcoat and straightened his cornflower blue silk tie.

"My dear lady, think nothing of it. Happens frequently."

An insouciant twinkle in his eye gave him a certain roguish look.

I had a gracious dwarf, with an engaging manner, in

my midst.

"Please sit down, how can I help you?" I pulled a fresh yellow legal pad towards me.

"What seems to be the problem?"

"I thought you were the one with the problem, my dear."

"Sorry?"

"I'm here to help you solve your problem."

"I don't have a problem. I'm an investigator, I solve problems." I was beginning to think I'd strayed into an alternative universe. One strewn with delusional dwarves.

"My dear friend, Ms Alexandra Struan indicated you had offered me a job."

My brain froze. The polar ice cap thawed slightly before absorbing this vital piece of information.

"I take it you're Quill?"

"Crammond McQuillan at your service. Quill to my friends."

Lexi's ex-con. The one she thought would be a perfect fit for my business. I don't mind admitting I wasn't quite seeing it. Still, I owed Lexi the honour of at least exploring further. Either that or I owed her a kick up the bahookie for putting me in this position.

"Would you like a cup of coffee?"

I might cope with this better if I had a shot of caffeine. Mainlined, preferably.

"Earl Gray tea, my dear."

The terms of endearment were beginning to get right up my bonnie Prussian nose. Our partnership would be short-lived if I didn't put him straight.

While this riveting exchange occurred my useless pet had cosied up to Quill. Head in the man's lap he gazed adoringly up at his new friend. I passed over a box of tissues. This love fest would involve a wet lap if it went on for too long. In an unfortunate place. Either that or the mutt would be ruining the poor man's marriage prospects.

I gave the situation some thought. Quill fondled Eagal's ear. The colours were still not pinned to the mast, about our future as a detective duo. Holmes and Watson, we were not. However, I was willing to give the man some leeway, given his choice of beverage. An ex-con who drinks Earl Grey must have some redeeming qualities. He had ten minutes to convince me before being heaved out the door. Time is money in my business.

"Lexi told me you have skills which I might find useful."

"I certainly do, my de—"

"Cass. Call me Cass."

"Whatever you say, Cass. Your wish is my command."

"These skills? What are they?"

Quill's loquaciousness was going to cost me big time. PI's should be brisk, succinct. If one used my mate Mike Hammer as a guide that is.

"I'm an expert safecracker and can enter any building you require without leaving a trace. I also do a nice line in creative accounting."

"What?"

My voice had taken on a falsetto quality I never knew existed. My abilities as a singer are nowhere near those of my talents as a ballerina. In fact, they are nowhere near anything you would call a song. That morning, however, my vocal cords were making a valiant attempt.

"I said—"

"I heard you. No. No way. This is a legitimate outfit. No burglars or fraudsters cluttering the place up."

"I'm new and improved. Ms Struan will testify to that. As will the prison chaplain."

I thought for a minute.

Quill watched me for several seconds and then said, "Besides, I'm brilliant."

"You can't be that brilliant. You've been in Perth Prison for the last year."

Quill nodded his head. Once. "Jake 'The Bomb' Halford cut a deal and ratted me out."

Honestly! How did Lex think any of this boosted my business?

"I'm not sure you're the right fit for the PI business."

His eyes narrowed, and I had the sudden urge to protect myself.

"I hope you're not alluding to my short stature?"

Bingo. I mean how expert would he be at covert surveillance? He'd stand out like a Scottie Dog in a box of Dalmatians.

"You don't blend in yourself. Not with hair like Basil Brush."

His argument was an excellent one. He didn't have to be so damn rude about it though.

I took the coward's way and said, "I alluded to your criminal past."

"How about this for a proposition? I've a little money stashed away. I can live on that for a few months. Give me a trial and I'll work for free."

Where the stash came from, I did not want to know. Still, turning down free labour was not in my remit.

I weighed up the options. Oh, what the heck. Us Claymores were also generous. Particularly to a fellow Scot behind the eight ball. The man had one chance.

Besides, there was talk of mysterious cash being bandied about.

"Deal, but a couple of rules."

"Anything." He adjusted his tie and smoothed back his hair. "Thank you my dea..."

He took in my look and coughed. "...Cass. You won't regret it."

"Rule number one, you will get expenses, but keep them to a minimum. The PI gig isn't paying that well yet."

He nodded vigorously. "Done. Cheap as I can."

"The second. No shenanigans. Nothing criminal whatsoever."

"What? But—"

"Not even a smidgeon of breaking and entering."

"Fine."

For his age, he didn't half take off a teenager well.

9

The office had a spare desk. My uncle had employed a young lass to answer the phone and do some filing. My accident occurred just as she reconsidered her options. She fancied the lawyer in the office downstairs and he had a position going. I took over her duties. When I inherited the firm, I moved my newly sharpened pencils over to the bigger desk. Solid oak and ancient, it looked the part.

I settled Quill into his new digs. "I'll find you a laptop. In the meantime, I need you to go to the library."

He hopped off his chair. Literally hopped off his chair. I handed him a yellow legal pad and a pen. "Pore through the Yellow Pages within a fifty-mile radius of Aberdeen. I need the names and numbers of every antiques dealer or auction house."

"Of course. I will leave no chuckie unturned. Your list will be thorough."

He didn't really need to go to the library. Yell.com would have suited our purposes. I wanted him gone. He left; I fished out my uncle's old laptop. I backed it up and wiped the hard drive. The backup nestled inside the safe, tucked away in a secret room. A switch underneath my desk triggered a bookcase to open. Tada! The best little hidey-hole a girl could inherit.

When my pint-sized associate returned, he would have his own username, password and squeaky-clean storage space. Then, one of the disadvantages of hiring an ex-con slammed into me like Mike Tyson's fist. My new employee's skills might include recovering all the data. In the time it took me to brew a decent pot of coffee. I picked up the phone.

"Lachie, can someone wipe Uncle Will's hard drive?"

"Why d'ya wanna wipe it? It'll be stuffed with info. You need all the help you can get."

My brother can be a right snob at times. He doesn't think much of me and my new career as a PI. Still, I needed his expertise so I tholed it.

I told him about my new assistant. Given Lachie's career, I omitted the bit about him being an ex-con.

"Wouldn't he find the info useful?"

"Stop interrogating me. Can you sort it or not?"

Years of letting me have my own way kicked in.

"I'll send someone round."

I scoured the net for likely places to dump a vintage teddy in exchange for a wad of cash. A half a dozen possible hidey holes had revealed themselves when the door flew open and assaulted the wall. A uniformed copper owned the space. His black hair, cut United States Marine issue, shouted new to the game. Most coppers round these parts had a soupcon of length. They didn't want a neon sign saying police, above their heads A huge Alsatian accompanied him. Cute in a mafia sort of way.

Eagal leapt up. One small growl from the interloper soon had him sitting down again. The police dog even spoke mafia. It would appear Lachie updated his chum as to my dog's personality. The Alsatian sat at attention and eyeballed Eagal. It was the gunfight at the OK Corral, canine style.

"The Sarge says you've something for me."

I handed him a laptop case.

Whipping it from my hand, he said, "I'll have it back in a couple of hours." He loped off, he and his canine companion setting a cracking pace.

Eagal gave one booming wuff as though saying good riddance. He slunk behind the desk, flopped down, and started snoring. The hectic life of a mountain dog in the confines of Bonnie Dundee. I made a note to actually take him up a mountain. Or at least a steep hill. Eagal without exercise is like a kid high on e-numbers.

Five minutes into my search Quill reappeared. He clutched a brand-new leather briefcase.

I sat back and shoved my hair out of my eyes.

"How have you had time to research all the info I asked for *and* go shopping?"

"Photocopied the relevant pages."

Maybe my pint-sized assistant's unique skills included ingenuity and brains.

"Go and buy sandwiches from the Scot Cafe. I'll have a vegetarian wrap."

I pulled my purse from the drawer.

"You'd be hard pushed to have anything else. They're not big on meat."

"I'm sure you'll find something."

I handed him twenty quid.

Peace reinstated itself.

He returned with the wrap, a huge baguette filled with what looked like a couple of chickens, a mixed salad and a brace of gargantuan slices of homemade lemon drizzle cake. He handed me ten pounds forty in change.

I peered at him, my eyes clouded with suspicion.

"How the dickens did you manage to buy that lot for nine pounds sixty? If you nicked a couple of sandwiches I swear—"

"I know you're a private investigator and all, but you need to keep that distrustful streak of yours under control."

"Stop prevaricating." I took a step towards him.

"The delightful young girl behind the counter did me a deal."

This was the first inkling I had of the effect Crammond McQuillan had on the opposite sex. I would be introduced to it many times during our professional relationship.

"And the chicken?"

"She nipped out to buy it for me."

Only Quill could come back from a vegetarian cafe with a sandwich stuffed with dead animal.

10

The United States Marine lookalike returned the laptop. Quill and I were knee deep in finding more suitable locations for offloading a vintage teddy. Or in Quill's case, thigh deep. The shrill ring of the phone startled us out of our task. We stared at it, me with sheer wonder. The first ring since I took ownership.

I reached out a hand and snatched it up. My hand trembled with excitement.

"Claymore Detective Agency, Cass Claymore speaking."

I listened, then, "Oh it's you."

I listened again. "No. No. I'm delighted to hear from you."

Another pause.

"See you soon."

I hung up and turned to the eager Quill.

"So, what's the job? Are we going to go on a stakeout? Chase a few crooks?"

"Take your spurs off, cowboy. Nothing like that. The Reverend Percy is coming for a visit."

"A minister? What does he want?"

"No clue. We'll find out when the Rev arrives."

I omitted to tell him one vital piece of information. I wanted to see the look on his face.

Twenty minutes later a raven-haired beauty walked into my office.Pregnant and wearing a dog collar she still exuded charisma. The Reverend Percy is my sister, Persephone. You may be sensing a hint of Classic Greek. My mother was a Greek Scholar before she fell into the loving arms of my father. Us girls all have names from Greek Mythology. Jocasta rounds up the trio. Cassandra means to excel or shine in Greek. Particularly fitting for my previous career where I shone like the brightest star. The matter was open to debate given my latest career. Lachie reckons I should change it to Artemis, the God of war. I'd agree trouble seems to follow me everywhere.

You'll notice my brothers all have Scottish names. Family rumour has it daddy refused to allow mythological names for the boys. No son of his would be called Apollo or Zeus. It was the only time he didn't allow my mother her own way. A jolly good thing. Growing up they'd have been hammered daily for having a poncy name.

I digress.

Quill leapt to his feet and moved swiftly over to Percy's side. He held out his hand.

"Who is this beautiful lady?"

The twinkle reasserted itself and I swear Percy simpered. He took her hand and kissed it. Percy melted in front of my eyes. What? My strong, independent big sister falling for the charms of a man other than her husband?

"The Reverend Percy Dunstable. A pleasure to meet you."

Her cheeks adopted a rosy glow.

"The pleasure is all mine."

The rosy glow intensified by about a gazillion watts.

A small voice diverted me from this vomit-inducing display.

"Hi, Auntie Cass."

Percy held the hand of a six-year-old, with missing teeth and a long tangle of carroty curls. My niece, Phoebe. She was the reason Eagal refrained from leaping around like a demented sprite. He turned into a lump of jelly the minute anyone under the age of 18 appeared.

I swept the child up in a hug and kissed her head, inhaling the fresh scent of strawberry shampoo. Her current favourite. Two weeks ago, it was bubble gum. Her arms were warm around my neck. Actually, everything was warm around my neck at the moment.

"Hello, beautiful. Why aren't you at school?"

Percy managed to drag herself away from Quill and turn her attention back to me.

"Her bit of the school's shut. Burst pipe according to her teacher. I need you to mind her for a couple of hours. A dying parishioner needs me up in Ninewells Hospital."

"No. No way. Take her to Mamah."

"Mamah's got a teaching gig at the University."

I opened my mouth. Before I uttered one word, she chipped in.

"I am not leaving her with Angus." She wagged a stern finger. "There'd be some sort of disaster and I don't want her following me up to Ninewells. The staff in A&E have enough on their hands without Claymore's cluttering the place up."

Percy's voice had taken on the no-nonsense tone of a minister dealing with a rowdy youth group. Knowing I was in a no-win situation, I gave in gracefully.

My sister left the child, a couple of colouring books, a packet of pencils, a small box of lego and the scent of lemon from her perfume.

While I wished Percy a fond farewell, her daughter

had transported herself to Quill's desk. She stared at him.

"You're small. I'm almost 's big as you. Why are you small?"

"Phoebe Dunstable, don't be so rude."

Quill smiled at her. "A good question young lady. The answer, I'm very special."

The man rose several notches in my estimation.

"Do you want to colour in with me?"

The Phoebe Dunstable stamp of approval.

"Much as I would love to, your aunt requires me to work. You can sit next to me."

He pulled the client chair out and helped her clamber up. She opened her colouring book and applied a red pencil well inside the lines.

"Good job, little one. I like the red."

That sounded odd coming from a dwarf.

"You speak funny. I like you."

Quill's smile put the sun to shame.

"I find I am also rather fond of you young lady."

I had inadvertently hired a childminder. Perhaps this assistant lark wouldn't turn out so bad.

Forty phone calls later we were hot, bored and no further forward. Even Phoebe chanted my spiel. I considered giving her my mobile and letting her have at it. Anything to make the list go down more quickly. No one owned up to having bought a teddy of any description. Without the sprog, I would have visited the stores. I thought about it for a few minutes. It wasn't such a bad idea.

One slight hiccup in my plan. I couldn't leave my sister's cherished progeny with an ex-con. Reformed or not he was still on remand and my sister expected me to cosset the sproglet.

A few permutations of a possible strategy cycled briskly through my mind. I decided.

"We're off out on a jaunt. Phoebe, let me put some sunscreen on you."

Ginger hair, equals pale complexion, equals several bottles of sun cream readily available.

"Quill you're coming as well. Grab a couple of bottles of water from the fridge."

I phoned my ever-helpful grandfather who agreed to babysit both the shaggy rug on legs and the office. He also agreed to lend me his car.

"You're one in a gazillion, Elgin Claymore."

"Don't you forget it, lassie."

The praise might be a tad effusive given the state of Grandad's car. More a lawnmower on wheels, it held together with rust, sticking plaster and prayer. The main thing it had going for it was no one would suspect a PI of driving one. Tramps more readily spring to mind.

Elgin appeared, sporting the sartorial look. He wore a pair of grey chinos, with crease so sharp they could qualify as a lethal weapon. A navy blazer, pink shirt and purple cravat completed the ensemble.

Quill snapped to attention.

"Sir, I can see you are a man of taste."

He held out his hand. "Crammond McQuillan. You may call me Quill."

Granddad gazed at Quill with an appraising eye. He smiled and shook hands.

"Aye, Quill. You're no' so bad yourself."

"Boys, much as your love in is enthralling me, there's work to be done."

There was a small delay in our departure. Pheobe wanted to stay with her beloved Grandpa, resulting in a lot of wailing, tears and clutching of legs. I remained resolute. Much as my grandfather acted like a youngster he was still an elderly man. He had enough with the Hound of The Baskervilles. Adding an excitable six-year-old to the mix might just lead to straws and camels being called to mind.

I managed to propel Phoebe out of the door by doing the mature adult thing. I told her she could have an ice-cream and a milkshake. These being her preferred food groups the tears magically vanished. She shoved her hat on her head at a jaunty angle and bounded out of the door. Bribery? You could bet Bart on it. I'm her aunt and had no qualms whatsoever about dosing her up with sugar. My health-conscious sister might have different views on suitable nutrition for her wee bairn. That was a worry for later.

I rooted a Disney CD out of the glove compartment and chucked it in the player. This kept Phoebe occupied singing along. To my amazement, Quill also knew all the words.

"Are they big on Disney in chokey?"

"Ha, flaming ha. I've a laddie of my own. At least I did until his mum dragged him stateside. I found out after the event."

The old noggin took a few minutes to process.

"Do you see him?"

He gave me the 'are you a halfwit' look. Or at least I imagine he did. Difficult to tell when your eyes are on the road ahead. He had cause, given his circumstances.

"I've only been out of prison a week. Not had much time to consider it."

"You will, though?"

To be honest I wasn't liking his chances. Former

choices up to now wouldn't appear virtuous on any application.

Quill apparently thought the same. "It's one of the reasons I've changed careers. My lifestyle doesn't lend itself to a strong application for access."

That very second, I realised I would give Quill a serious go. He needed this job and would give it his all.

Initiate warp speed immediately for agency growth.

My decision meant responsibility for an employee. The Claymore Detective Agency now had two full-time members of staff. It felt good. Mind you, not that good that I wouldn't take him up on his offer of a couple of months' free labour. The end of his penal servitude would see him signing a contract. Provided we stayed in business.

11

We all tumbled out of the car in a leafy suburb of Aberdeen. A pungent scent of lavender mounted a stealth attack on our nostrils. Someone had trouble sleeping. By the size of the houses, and the glut of Lamborghinis, I couldn't imagine anyone having trouble sleeping.

"Phoebe, keep your hands to yourself in the shop."
  She nodded, a grave look on her face.
  "I'm helping you 'vestigate. I'll be all growed up, Auntie Cass."
  "I'm sure you will poppet. Just in case hold my hand and put the other one in your pocket."

She complied without a murmur. Her hand felt soft and warm in mine. Thank heavens it wasn't Hezekiah, her brother, who accompanied me. His bit of the school didn't have a burst pipe, so he was still safely ensconced in the building. If I say Hezzie and Eagal are twins when it comes to behaviour, then you'll get a general idea of the vibrancy of his personality. I love him to Mars and back, but three seconds in his company reduces me to quivering wreck status. If he were involved, I would be up to my pert little bottom in damage claims.

The shop could have been lifted from an Agatha Christie novel. Perfect in a leafy English village, but not an Aberdeen suburb. All lead windows and medieval lettering. A skull glared at me as I walked past. I fought the urge to recite, "Alas poor Yorick."

Quill hesitated then hurried past the window. For an ex-con he's a right feardie.

Phoebe stared in the window, transfixed.

"What's that, Auntie Cass?"

"I'll tell you later." I yanked her into the shop.

"Ow. That hurted."

"Sorry, poppet."

Several shops and a few false alarms later, my wee assistant investigator had had enough. Phoebe that is, not Quill. Ready to take on the world, he strode ahead. Prison gave you stamina over and above the ordinary motorbike riding PI

Out of the nine shops visited, five were selling teddies. Even I, with my limited grasp of antiquities, could tell they were fakes.

I resolved to add a book on antiques to the bookshelves in my office. The book stash was the one thing I kept of my uncle's, apart from the computers and his files. Somewhat lacking in the finer side of antique collecting, it needed an upgrade. It looked like a crash course might be imminent. This investigating lark was harder than it appeared. My intensive knowledge of ballet and classical music had limited use. Not unless a break-in at the local dance school got thrown my way. Or a local record shop.

I digress. Again. Seems to be my strongest point.

The conversation in most of the shops went something like this.

"I'm looking to purchase a Steiff bear with tan fur."

Phoebe adopted the pathetic, or excited, look as the mood took her. We had an actress in the family. The wee darling. I might employ her more often.

43

"Of course, Madam." The dealer turned and walked towards a display cabinet.

Shop six had an added extra. I stared, hypnotized, as the dealer's toupee slipped down his head.

Without missing a beat, he lifted his hand and moved it back into place, repeated roughly every thirty seconds. It left me wondering if you could buy anything to keep a wig in place. My investigator's mind churns with such important details.

I whipped the iPhone from my pocket and tapped a few keys. I was improving at this doing things surreptitiously business. Mike Hammer would be proud. It turned out wig tape was a thing. I wondered if I should let the man know. Nah.

I snapped off a few hurried photos while I had the phone out. Why, I didn't know. It's what most PI's would do and I'm learning as I go along. I was one up on the pulp fiction detectives as they didn't have mobile phones. They did have photographic memories though.

The man returned carrying a couple of bears. Both had the button in the ear, but not the original. They were also the wrong colour. I might not be the brightest PI on the block, but I knew enough to research Steiff. This meant I understood as much, if not more, as your average dodgy antiques dealer.

I picked up one of the bears. Wig man glared at me.

"Madam, do not touch the merchandise."

"My man, one needs to make an informed decision as to which is the best."

Speaking hoi polloi was considered a critical skill at the Royal Ballet.

"Perhaps the little lady should decide?"

44

I handed the bear to Phoebe. The man snatched it back only a millimetre from the wean's waiting hands.

She burst into tears. More hunger than genuine distress at the loss of the bear. She could supply every shop in Scotland with soft toys. I carted her outside.

I turned around at the door. "How dare you treat a child like that."

Wig man didn't seem too bothered. He looked more like something rotten had been dragged in.

"Those bears were fakes," I informed my assistants who appeared somewhat underwhelmed by my pronouncement.

"You seem to know a lot about antique bears for someone who's only just hung up their shingle."

"I've mastered Google."

"Enlighten me, my dear."

I decided to let the 'my dear' remark go. I didn't want every conversation with Quill to turn into a battle.

"No markings on the button in ear. Bart's had the original elephant, so truly vintage. That one didn't even say Steiff."

"Ooh, aren't you the clever girl."

"I'm also a fashion guru. That bear was neither alpaca nor mohair."

"I can see I need to study makes of bears. Anything else?"

"Study everything, not just bears."

"About the bears?" Quill's efforts to avoid eye-rolling were obvious.

"Apart from the fact that Bart is tan, no nothing. Those two were chocolate and grey. Totally wrong colour for our missing teddy."

The tears miraculously stopped when we stepped outside. We headed towards the ice cream shop. Phoebe declared she would like strawberry, toffee and chocolate ice cream. I wasn't so sure about three scoops.

12

Quill entertained our charge by reciting Dr Seuss, as we strolled towards Scoopy Doo's. The munchkin skipped along, leaving me to my own thoughts. These were leading me to believe we should go and speak to Lady Lucy again. Interrogating her husband also featured.

Phoebe, the elfin extortionist, managed to inveigle three scoops of ice cream and a cake out of me. That girl had a future in the FBI. By the time we'd finished, she bounced around the room like a hyperactive Tigger.

"Yummy! 'Snice eating ice cream. My very favourite kind. I like being with you, Auntie Cass. Better 'n school."

She drew a deep breath then carried on.

"Where next? Quill, are you going to stay with us? I want you to. You're fun. More fun than my brothers."

Maybe my sister was right about the effect sugar had on her darling daughter.

I wondered whether I could put the cost of all the sugar against expenses. Lucinda had oodles of money and a few scoops of ice cream wouldn't break her bank. It might crucify mine.

While Phoebe wolfed down her snacks I made a quick phone call to Lachie. I gave him the tip about the dodgy antiques dealer.

"I'm in Dundee, Cass. What do you expect me to do about it?"

"Now that you're Police Scotland aren't you meant to dash off wherever you're needed."

The police in Scotland are now one humongous happy family. My brother had been swept up into the bosom, along with the rest of them.

"Flogging fake teddies isn't exactly international terrorism. I'll pass it on to Aberdeen."

"Your grumpiness increases with your age, Lachlan Claymore."

"Only with bratty little sisters." I could hear the smile in his voice.

Whatever he did, I could relax in the fact my duty as a concerned citizen was done.

Several more antiques shops were visited. One ran us out with a couple of pit bulls. I snatched Phoebe up and we hot-footed it. The dogs were stopped by one word from the equally vicious-looking man in charge of them. I was relieved on several fronts, the key one being I didn't fancy Quill's chances of outrunning a couple of dogs.

"He's not very friendly for someone running a shop."

"I recognised those pit bulls. They belong to Liam Laughlin. He uses them for dog fights."

"Isn't that illegal?"

"Of course, it is. Feel free to tell him. I value my life too much."

"Was the dog whisperer Liam?"

"No idea. I am not acquainted with the gentleman."

"You seem to retain a lot of info about someone you've never met."

"In my line of work, it pays to know the opposition." His voice dropped. "Especially if the opposition is Liam Laughlin."

13

We returned to the office tanned and footsore, but none the wiser as to Bart's whereabouts. Teddies, tan, Steiff, or otherwise, were in short supply.

Percy lounged in my office chair, drinking tea and chatting to Grandad.

"I hope you have not had my daughter involved in any shady business?"

"For a woman of the cloth, you don't trust many people."

"No, Cass. I don't trust *you*."

"Percy, I know you're a Claymore, but no need to wield one."

"Mummy we've had ice cream. Three scoops. Cake as well. And milk shake." Phoebe's delight in the unexpected treat meant it would not slip under the radar.

Bother. I could tell from Percy's narrowed eyes that this matter would be discussed further. At some point in the future. In detail. I didn't even want to think about what my sister could dream up as a punishment. Experience told me it would not be pretty. She favours the grittier passages from the Bible.

"How delightful, darling. Auntie Cass is very generous."

Her tone implied she meant stupid.

I changed the subject from my foibles as an appropriate guardian. Or I would have done if the door had not flown open, allowing entrance to what cheap books would describe as a blousy blonde. She had a face a model would die for and the personality of a pit bull who'd swallowed a wasp. Her balletic figure now resembled a barrage balloon on steroids.

My nemesis. Our relationship had never been chipper. It chucked itself off a cliff when I beat her to a scholarship with the Royal Ballet. Mimosa could bear a grudge like a Mafia Don. Her parents misnamed her. Hemlock would be more appropriate. Why on earth had she reappeared in my life after fifteen years?

I sneezed. She'd brought a strong whiff of designer finest with her.

"Mimosa, how delightful to see you."

"Cut it, Claymore. If you think you're forgiven, then you're more stupid than you were at school."

Her nose had the sort of tilt that indicated all those unfortunate enough to be anywhere in her orbit had rolled in something nasty.

Charming. How come the one woman I would beg Eagal to bury was the first one he blithely snored through? As an inheritance, he continued to prove useless.

"What do you want then?" My voice held a hint of Russian temper.

"I need your help."

"*My* help? Since when have you ever asked me for help?" I glowered at her for good measure. Seems to me it's what I should be doing as a PI - looking hard.

Her look indicated she thought I was glaikit rather than hard. For those of you not blessed to speak Scottish, it means idiot.

"You run a detective agency, don't you? I need you to detect."

Another client. Or was it? My mercenary side duelled with my get stuffed side. Mercenary won.

I kicked Percy and Phoebe out for reasons of client confidentiality. Granddad decided to go with them and eat tea at Percy's.

"I'll catch you up. Want a wee word with your sister," he informed her.

Suspicion clouding her eyes, Percy gathered up her daughter and all her accoutrements.

"Bye, Auntie Cass." A quick hug and my wee detective pal trotted behind her mother. My sister's ramrod back gave her the look of an Old Testament prophet.

It turned out Mimosa's brother, Florian, was missing. For four days. The police thought he'd gone off somewhere and would reappear at a time of his own choosing. From what I knew of him they were doubtless right. He was more hapless than my brother, Angus, and that's not an easy feat. If Florian were my brother, I'd encourage him to disappear. Still, if she wanted to pay me …

Due to the fact Mimosa was a cantankerous besom, dealing with her daily would be classed as a hazardous occupation. I upped my fees. That and the fact she had gone into high finance after her disappointment in the field of ballet. Rumour had it, Andrew Carnegie could tap her for a loan.

The truth of this became clear as she handed over a a cheque for four thousand pounds. Without complaint. Blimey. Maybe this detecting gig would turn out to be bountiful. If I bumped up all my fees like that, future detecting could be done between trips to the Galapagos.

Quill moved in for a moment of schmoozing and I could swear she smiled before she left. It reminded me of a rabid Rottweiler, but a smile nonetheless. I studied her eyes carefully. Yep, a definite widening of the old peepers. My assistant did, indeed, possess skills I required.

"Anything happen while I was out?"

Maybe a rhetorical question given that Grandad had stayed behind to have a cosy chat.

He straightened his tie and his posture. I waited for something momentous given the grandeur of the rearranging. Instead, he handed me an envelope.

"This came for you."

I hid my disappointment for Grandad's sake and tore open the envelope. Out slid a sheet of paper. I stared at its contents. Cliche it may be, but I held a warning note in my hand. Complete with obligatory words cut out of newspapers. You'd think the local thugs could be more imaginative. The words it contained left little to my imagination.

You're playing a dangerous game.
Death the only outcome.
Drop your case.

The envelope also contained a photograph of a gun. Not torn from a newspaper. A photo of a real live gun. Presumably owned by someone. What had I stumbled in to? How could the loss of an auld teddy lead to implied threats and illegal firearms? At least I assumed they were illegal. Scottish Law means that anyone caught with a gun, who wasn't at an official shooting club, would spend a long time at Her Majesty's pleasure.

I was fast regretting my career choice. Guns weren't part of my vision for the future of Claymore Detective Agency. Neither was dying. I hadn't escaped death at the hands of a drunkard just to be offed in a spectacular manner in Dundee.

14

Feeling my blood pressure drop, I sank down into a chair like a heroine in a historical melodrama. Sank is the wrong word for it. No graceful swoon, but a good old Dundee thump. Dear old granddaddy rushed to my aid. I swear if he had smelling salts they would be wafting under my nose. Lacking the necessary salts, he resorted to the only other method of resuscitating a Victorian heroine. Slapping me on the face.

Despite the brutality, it had the desired effect. My blood pressure rocketed into the stratosphere. I followed it.

"Enough of that. No guns. And no slapping. Ever."

The squeak in my voice woke Eagal who leapt up and started barking.

"I was worried—"

"Guns? What's all this about guns?" Quill had caught the falsetto train.

My office had turned into the inner sanctum of hell. Everyone leapt about shouting. Well not quite everyone. I sat down again and yelled. "Quiet."

Both obedience and silence were immediate. Apart from the mutt, who dashed in my direction barking even louder. I shoved him away. Forcefully. This had the effect of him careening towards Quill, who got knocked down in the charge.

He jumped up, unbloodied, and fondled Eagal's ears. "Enough boy. Hush now." The barking stopped.

How come everyone but me can control the *Hound of the Baskervilles'* spawn.

The silence lasted about 30 seconds before the dog's pea size brain kicked in and instructed him to bark again. Louder.

"We're going to hell in a helicopter." Grandad's grasp of vernacular never failed to astonish me. He didn't so much speak English as reinvent it.

"It's hell in a handbasket."

"What does it mean, anyway. Stupid saying."

He had a point. I've no clue what the original means either. Neither did I have the time or energy to work it out. Too busy going to hell in a hurry.

The door flew open and bounced off the wall. The lawyer from downstairs exploded through the gap, flaky receptionist treading his heels.

"Shut that bloody animal up or I swear I'll make sure you're evicted." The lawyer's tone was stern. And loud.

The receptionist had nothing to add to the conversation. Her only task appeared to be looking beautiful, in a flowery dress and Doc Martin boots. That and grasping his arm. Who the freak wears Doc Martin's in a heatwave? The rest of us wore the minimum we could get away with and still stay legal.

In case you're wondering this is a mixed-use building. By this I mean, as well as having a resident lawyer, the top floor's occupied by a loan shark. At least I think he's a loan shark. I've not mustered up the mettle to ask. Some dodgy looking characters trail up the stairs. Yes, even more dodgy than the lot that hang about here. I bet some of Quill's mates visited.

I busied myself feeding treats to the pooch in a bid to stop the clamour. Multitasking is not his forte.

Quill loped over and snatched the paper from my

hand.

He took one look and slowly backed against the wall. His face said he was going to follow me with the slumping, sinking or thumping.

"I thought you were a hot-shot crook? After a year in the clink, you should be used to guns."

"Thieving was my game. Nary a gun to be seen."

I wished there was nary a gun to be seen in my game either. Jobseekers looked enticing to me.

"What's up with you lot?"

I stepped outside the case long enough to check out he of the sexy voice. Tall, unruly hair, stubble, gangly and with a prominent Adam's apple. The type of man most women would pass over. Until he smiled. This transformed him into Adonis. It also turned his eyes from River Tay grey to electric blue. Thoughts of Larbert rushed from my mind as I realised why the secretary had defected.

"Cass Claymore," I said, my voice weak.

His touch, as he shook my hand, sent shockwaves up to my brain. A firm shake of the head helped to dislodge the fog that had taken up residence there.

"Simon Baring. You look like your favourite cat's just died."

"We're good." No way I was blabbing about this case. Not to lawyers who could turn on the charm.

The smile disappeared, and gangly, slate grey reappeared. "Keep that dog of yours under control. I'm sure there are rules on bringing dogs to work."

He and Doc Martin left for quieter pastures. This left me with a feeling of wanting to stuff his help right up his electric blues.

Great. Now I had a lawyer with a grudge on my case. How much more could a budding PI take. The answer to that - a lot more. I'm a Claymore. Not only that, ballet taught you to hang in when the going got tough. That was the difference between a dancer in the corps de ballet and a soloist.

Saying all that, hanging in when guns are involved is a whole different game from learning an adagio sequence in ballet. That was simple mathematics. The worst that could happen was an injury. Not much threat to life. Although most ballerinas, me included, thought their life was over when their ballet career ended. None of them remotely imagined they'd end up running a low-end Scottish detective agency.

This left me pondering what to do next.

"Elgin, you need to go join Percy before she comes storming in here."

"No way."

"Yes, way. And don't go blabbing to the rest of the family. This is 'need to know' stuff. No one else needs to know."

"Your father needs to know."

"Tell him and I'll be using one of his guns on you. You're an employee of this firm, so confidentiality rules apply."

"Employed? Show me the colour of your money."

I pulled a fiver out of my pocket and slammed it on the desk in front of him."

"There."

"Cheapskate."

"I'm barasic. It'll buy you and your mate a pint down the legion."

A blank contract followed the five-pound note. I filled it in. "Here. Sign this." It had a confidentiality clause Houdini couldn't wriggle out of.

He obliged with a twinkle in his eyes. Picking up his pay he winked, then departed for the Rev's car.

Quill had recovered from his shock over the guns.

You'd think employing a criminal he'd keep me safe. Looked like it would be the other way around. A word with Lexi was fast becoming the order of the day. She'd saddled me with an assistant with specialist skills. Now it turned out those skills were severely lacking. I wondered if she'd trade him in for an upgraded model. One that could also double as a bodyguard.

"How come I've not got one of those?" he enquired politely.

"Fiver or contract?"

"Both."

I gave into the inevitable, slipped him a fiver and filled another contract out. He signed it with a fountain pen and a flourish. More eye twinkling.

"You are a true lady, Cassandra Claymore. I am delighted to be of service to you and look forward to our continuing working relationship."

Grief. Would this bloke ever shut up? I was fast regretting our continuing relationship, working or otherwise.

"Quill, you really need to work on shortening your sentences. Clipped. To the point. Matter of fact." I tapped the desk to emphasise each point. "That's what's needed."

"Of course. I will comply forthwith."

I shook my head and gave up.

Some detective agency this was turning out to be. A ballet dancer, a dwarf and an octogenarian. Even I wouldn't employ my services.

There was no escaping the fact someone had engaged my services. Two someones who were obviously intelligently challenged. So, I needed to investigate. Like my sign said – 'Claymore's always deliver'. At this rate, it would be pizza delivery. But I owed this investigating lark every atom of my being.

15

"I'm retiring to partake of a small libation. Will you join me?"

"If you mean you're off to the pub, then no. I've got to walk the four-legged explosion."

"That dog's so big it needs its own postcode."

"I think he might be taking a dirt nap sometime soon. He eats as much as my entire postcode."

"You sound like a New York mobster."

He gazed at the mutt, an adoring look in his eyes.

"Poor Eagal. He's a wee topper."

Eagal pricked up one ear at the mention of his name. It soon flopped down again, the effort being too much for him.

"You keep him for a week. You'll soon change your mind." I was rapidly becoming a tad fed up with all this admiration for my brain-dead pooch.

"You need to come and visit the public house with me. It will be enlightening."

"Which public house would that be?"

"The Duck and Dagger."

"You made that up."

"I can assure you, Madam, the establishment exists."

"How come I've never heard of it?"

"It is not the sort of business you would ordinarily frequent."

My hackles rose. What was my employee dragging me in to? He elaborated.

"It's in the docks. Let's say it's mostly unsavoury characters who hang out there."

I opened the drawer and pulled out Eagal's lead. "No way. I'll see you tomorrow."

"I insist. There are some people I would like you to meet."

"I do the insisting, and meeting and greeting, round here."

My natural curiosity soon got the better of me. Plus, I appreciated any self-respecting PI would follow every lead, no matter how repulsive. I needed to buckle up, and maybe not enjoy the ride but at least take it.

"Fine, I'll meet you there at seven."

"Can you pick me up?"

I wondered who the employee was around here.

Before heading to the delights of a night with my assistant, shopping beckoned. The mutt got through double his body weight in food every day, and I needed more veggies. How was I to know there was a worldwide shortage of kale? Seven supermarkets in and I found the last one standing. So did two other women, a nun, and a lone man, inexplicably dressed as a cowboy. Kale being a staple food group in Scotland, it was elbows at dawn. With a deft pirouette serving to scatter the competition, I grabbed the kale. One wrinkled worthy, showing spunk not seen since World War 1, wrestled it from my hands. In the resulting fracas, I got four leaves, a black eye and a lifetime ban from Tesco. I picked up a cabbage and decided a different type of shake was needed.

Using the motorbike perhaps wasn't the brightest thing I'd ever done. A four-foot man on the back of a motorbike is a sight to behold, so I'll leave it to your imagination. By dint of judicious holding on we made it to our destination. I don't want to mention some of the places he was holding on. I was willing to give him the benefit of the doubt re his reasons for this. Quill nearly toppled me off a couple of times so our progress was not smooth. I'm surprised I didn't get hauled over for drunk driving as that was the impression I gave. Even Lachy might screw his nose up at that one.

16

The clientele wasn't the only unsavoury thing about The Duck and Dagger. The building was an eyesore. The main things keeping it upright were peeling paint, Graffiti and the punters who packed the place out. The smoking ban hadn't made it to this corner of Dundee. I felt like a real PI at last.

"This dump takes the word pigsty and elevates it to a whole new level of awfulness."

"Methinks the lady doth protest too much."

"The lady's your boss. She can protest as much as she likes."

I coughed my way through the fug to the bar. Ordering a whisky, I slugged it down and coughed with renewed vigour.

Quill materialized at my side.

"You know you can't drive now you've had that?"

Sod it, I'd forgotten the zero-tolerance limit on Alcohol. I was stuck here until the spirits wore off. I didn't even like whisky but fitting in has its down sides. The place was wall to wall bikers, all tension, testosterone and tattoos, and that was just the women. The men looked like they'd recently broken out of Alcatraz. I needed a minder, not a wee dram of Highland Nectar.

Quill dragged me over to a gaggle of seven bikers standing in the corner. Crosses adorned their leathers. At least the ones I could see did. My assistant strode up to them and it was manly hugs all round. The participants ranged from dwarf to giant making it a sight to behold. I stood back, looking both stupid and surplus to requirements.

Ritual completed, Quill turned to me.
"These gentlemen are the reason I changed my ways."
I raised a questioning eyebrow.
"They visited me in the prison. Helped me when my boy quit the country."
The tallest of the bunch stepped forward and held out his hand. "I'm Stuart, the leader of this motley crew. Spiritual leader that is. We're part of the CMA."
He took in my puzzled look.
"Christian Motorcycle Association."
Through the morass of my synapses, I remember Percy lauding the organisation. I thought she was joking.
"I don't mean to be rude, but wouldn't I be better hobnobbing with the other lot. They're more likely to give me useful intel."
The bikers burst out laughing.
"We've more insight than you give us credit for, lass."
Unshaven, with hair of a length that rivalled mine, I was wont to believe him. In fact, I wondered if he'd wandered in from the opposition. The scar twisting the corner of his mouth sealed my impression and gave his smile a wonky downturn. Sexy in a rough boy way.

Whilst this enlightening conversation took place, the atmosphere from the remainder of the pub was palpable. Dark and brooding, it loomed over us like Storm Anaconda or whatever the current name for a hurricane might be.
I fast came to realise the duck part of the pub's name meant evading an errant dagger rather than webbed feet

fowl. Quill was looking at a swiftly delivered P45 for dragging me into this.

I glowered back at the assembled company in an attempt to look brave. My shiny new leathers gave away my uninitiated status, so I made a mental note to rough them up. Maybe I should have bought second-hand.

Chewing on my lip, I cogitated on whether my hair would look better in a ponytail? Who the heck knew what a real biker chick looked like. Certainly not me.

I took in the other birds in the room. Impressive sleeve tattoos featured in their appearance. I decided going down the ink route was taking things a step too far for me, despite my desire to fit in.

My eyes flickered towards the exits thinking I might make my escape. Then I remembered I was incarcerated until the drink wore off. Bummer.

Deciding to make the most of things I said in a loud voice, "Anyone seen a vintage teddy being hawked around the bazaars. The stupidity of my statement hit me square between the eyes before the words were out of my mouth.

It struck me I'd used a much louder voice than I thought. The chatter stopped around me then silence rippled around the room. About a hundred and twenty-three pairs of eyes swivelled towards me. They indicated two things. Quite clearly. What sort of pansy biker worried about teddies, and where did this deranged chick come from?

The looming became more physical than emotional. In fact, it was the type of looming that could become assault and battery at the twitch of an upturned lip. Or the uttering of one more stupid question. Bravery only took me so far. I stepped back, and they loomed further.

I gained a thorough comprehension of what Quill meant when he said the characters inside the Duck and Dagger were mostly unsavoury.

Just as I considered fleeing and taking my chances with drink driving, Stuart stepped forward and whispered in my ear. "I hope you've plenty money."

I gulped, nodded, and waited for the next move in the fast-developing potential riot.

Stuart turned to the crowd and said with a wide grin and an expansive wave of his hands, "Cass here tells me the next round's on her."

He slapped me on the back so hard I stumbled forward. Fortunately, towards the bar. With visions of my fast draining bank account flying around my head, I pulled out my debit card and meekly handed it over.

I discovered two things. Most of the bikers were on lemonade and the Duck and Dagger's prices were ridiculously cheap. Low-profit margins were probably the reason for the pub's general air of neglect. That and the fact riots might feature within these hallowed walls. Redecorating would be a complete waste of time.

Quill leaned nonchalantly against the bar taking in the crowd. For a non-biker, he didn't half seem at home. He now sported brand new leathers. To be honest, despite his attire being cleaner than mine, he looked a hundred times more at home. He also managed to look his usual sartorial self. It would not surprise me if he had a shirt and time on under his jacket. Come to think of it, why wasn't he dying of heat exhaustion. He was the only one in the bar wearing his jacket. Quill, as always, remained a mystery to me.

"When in the name of the blessed Saint Percy did you find time to buy those duds?"

"I took a trip to the bike shop in Broughty Ferry. They managed to kit me out with the minimum of fuss."

Top of the range, these didn't come cheap. My assistant's finances bothered me to an extent that I expected the blue light brigade to come knocking at the door. Handling stolen money was not how I wanted my business to be remembered.

"This little nest egg you've got squared away, how big is it?"

He looked suddenly shifty, his gaze darting around the room. "Shhh. Are you trying to get me killed?"

I lowered my voice. "Sorry, it's just you've invested in a briefcase and biker gear today. Splashing the cash seems to be natural in your orbit."

"My dad left me some money in his will."

His innocent look did not fool me. There was more to this than met the eye.

"Where did your late lamented daddy get the money?"

I knew I would regret asking.

"Let's just leave it at the fact I joined the family business."

Dear God, what had I got myself into. From the Royal Ballet to smoky pubs and professional criminal assistants. Not a stellar career progression. I pondered how much further could I fall?

No wonder my mother didn't approve of the change in my lifestyle. Boasting to your pals about a daughter playing the lead in Swan Lake is far superior to muttering she's a dodgy PI

Even I had to agree. A daft adventure only takes a body

so far before reality hits like a Harley Davidson Road King. Hard and fast.

17

I hitched a ride home on the back of a bike. After several whiskies, I didn't care whose bike, so I think my knight in shining leathers was more of a Hell's Angel than one of his Christian counterparts. The only thing I remember about the journey is hanging on tightly whilst singing Bat Out of Hell a la soprano. I'm surprised he didn't dump me in the docks.

Shug, at least I think that was his name, opened my door and shoved me through. I landed in an ungainly heap. He lobbed the keys inside after me, slammed the door, and left. He was probably glad to get shot of the singing detective and re-evaluating his future as a gallant knight.

Contemplating sleeping where I lay, Eagal's tongue brought me back to rude realization of my plight. Whilst he licked, something battered off my head. I shoved him away and dragged myself upright. The hound from hell wore a wooden collar. A huge wooden collar. With ragged edges. My canine wrecking ball had been at it again.

"Eagal? What the freak have you been up to?"
Eagal's response involved a lot of barking and chewing on my leathers.
"Get off you stupid mutt."
I bent down and examined his latest collar. It was a lump of wood, the colour of which bore a distinct resemblance to my new sitting room door.

"You are in serious danger of becoming food for your mates."

Eagal didn't seem too worried about his plight or his fate. He pranced around like a six-year-old.

Standing up I staggered towards the sitting room, which now had an air-conditioned door. Turning back to the dog I noticed he had blood running from his ear. The idiot was so thick this did not appear to bother him. It had to bother me. I picked up the phone and dialled Alexander's number.

He wasn't best pleased and told me so in no uncertain terms. His argument seemed to be that the hours between midnight and 6 a.m. were for sleeping. This included 2.07 a.m. which, he said, was when I called him.

I was too busy drowning the whisky in buckets of water to take in most of his speech. By the time he'd sorted out Eagal and given me instructions on antibiotics most of his precious sleeping time had gone. Even in my befuddled state, I knew informing him that less speaking and more working would find us all on bed more quickly was an idiotic suggestion.

Alexander could be a right mardy so and so at times. I swear the nurses swapped him at the hospital when he was born. In a family of eccentrics, he remained uptight and reserved. Still, he came in useful as a free vet and spent as much time in the bosom of his family as the rest of us. Only a true Claymore would do that. Trust me, if you met my family you'd understand.

Eagal decided he was sleeping in my bed. This consisted of him taking nine-tenths of the total area. I got a sliver of what he left, the remainder being no man's land. It didn't stay this way for long as the pooch played the injured card and utilised the whole bed. After the third time of slamming to the floor, I grabbed a spare duvet and headed for the sofa. My flat might have five bedrooms, but it was deficient on the bed front. I needed to remedy that if the pooch stayed. The jury remained out on our shared living arrangements. Getting rid of him was cheaper than investing in a four-poster with a memory foam mattress.

Even without my furry comforter, my dreams were still littered with mad bikers wielding skulls in one hand and whisky in the other. A skeleton joined in and gave me a ride home on the back of a red Tiger 800 ABS, whilst I swigged champagne from a crystal flute and sang Hit the Road Jack.

18

I awoke to knocking. Loud knocking. Whether in my head or at the door was subject to debate. Swinging my feet to the ground I heaved myself upwards and staggered forwards.

"Okay. Okay."

The thundering continued until I pulled the door open. My brother, Angus, stood there sporting nothing but a smile and a pair of frayed denim shorts. His hair was pulled back in a ponytail which reached his waist. More bone idleness than a fashion statement. It was too much effort to go and get it cut. He carried a battered toolbox, making my heart sink.

"Alexander said you needed a few repairs done."

When I got my hands on Alexander he'd be in need of a wooden box and Percy's services. This took revenge too far.

Angus was the type of bloke who'd demolish a load-bearing wall whilst hanging a picture and break his finger in the process. He did three weeks of an SVQ in Painting and decorating before being kicked off as a health and safety hazard. The college didn't think their insurance premiums could handle his continued presence in the building.

He strode inside and followed instructions to sit on the sofa and not move. To the letter. When I returned with coffee for him and a shake for me, he was under the duvet and fast asleep.

Squinting at my watch I discovered I had time for a quick workout before heading for the office. I left the shake lying idle, safe in the knowledge that the shaggy waste disposal wouldn't go anywhere near it. If he wasted my precious kale he'd be on a one-way ticket to adoption.

Dragging Eagal out of bed proved an impossible task. He scraped at the plastic collar of shame protecting his neck, threw me a look that could kill kittens, and turned his back on me.

I resorted to that time-worn trick, opening a packet of cheese. Eagal's turbocharged slide into the kitchen sent him skidding on the parquet floor, resulting in me hurtling into a cupboard.

"You stupid mutt. I'm sending you to a puppy farm.'

The miscreant, too busy biting the cheese packet, didn't care about his future.

I snapped off a small piece, gave him it and put the rest in the fridge whilst he ate. Then locked it. Yep, that's right. The only way to keep food safe from my canine garbage tip was to have it under lock and key.

He settled down to a gargantuan breakfast while I showered and got dressed. A visit to the Laird beckoned so I needed to scrub up. However, I also needed to take the bike so much thought went into my outfit. This took me as a far as wearing a skirt and changing into leathers for the ride. I was beginning to realise a motorbike might not be the best mode of transport for a PI. Not in summer, where any self-respecting investigator was likely to die of heat exhaustion wearing the right kit. Hang on! This was Scotland. Summer would be over by the end of the week.

I left a note for Angus. It gave explicit instructions to

take the door off the hinges and take it to the dump. He was to do nothing else. I wasn't holding out any great hopes he would obey, but at least I tried.

Eagal was also in the mood for seeking revenge. For the outrage of the collar. He ran me to work via Menzieshill, before heading down to the river. The polar opposite to where I wanted to be. A pulp fiction detective would have had the four-legged fiend heading in the right direction and begging for mercy. I, on the other hand, spent most of the journey thinking about using running shoes for the walk to work in future.

I wondered if obedience classes would help.

19

My Aunty Morag wielded a mop like a gladiator preparing the Coliseum for a pride of lions and a brace of Christians. A very elegant gladiator. Her clothing choice for the job included the names, Versace and Jimmy Choo. I wasn't so much concerned about that as the fact she wielded her mop in my locked office.

"Your father said you could do with a wee hand."

More like he'd sent her to spy.

"The office is pristine, you've done a grand job."

As I spoke I relieved her of the mop and shooed her out the door.

I needed to retrieve that spare key from my dad. Too many relatives cluttering the place up. We'd be solving crimes by committee at this rate. Unless they were useful, of course. That was a whole nother crime solving scenario.

What's that you say? Why didn't I relieve Aunty Morag of the key? No way she was giving it up, so I might as well save my breath to cool my porridge.

Quill still hadn't made an appearance. Being late after only a couple of days on the dime did not a happy Cassandra make.

Pulling out Florian's file, I flipped it open with a nonchalant finger. I was practising insouciance, a required skill for a PI According to the penny dreadfuls where I did most of my research. I mused. Musing is also a required skill and I found myself pretty good at

75

this. How difficult could it be to find a missing person? Surely not that hard? Florian was most likely snuggled up in bed in the Bahamas. Lying next to his girlfriend, a brunette with legs up to her armpits and a tan a redhead could only dream of. Saying that, she'd have to have the intelligence of a forty-watt bulb to go out with Florian. His intelligence lay somewhere in the region of the ten-watt level.

Through brain fog, I remembnered asking the Christian bikers if they knew anything about his whereabouts. They replied in the negative. Things got hazier at that point but moseying on up to the Hell's Angels who littered the room, featured. Whisky loosened their tongues and gave them a rosier outlook towards me. I'd have to revisit when sober. My ability to retain information might be sharper.

You may be wondering why I asked a pub full of bikers about the missing Florian. It's a good question given there wasn't even a sniff of biker in the lad's description. Here's the thing. It's been said that Dundee is the biggest village in the world. I'd agree. It could certainly teach the Chinese a thing or two about whispers. If you sneezed in Balumbie by the time the news reached Menzieshill you would have pneumonia and weren't expected to live the night. There was a good chance that one of them knew my mark. The only problem I had, I couldn't remember a flaming thing about last night. Except cuddling Mr Leathers, of course. I remembered that clear as a bell. Unfortunately.

Quill appeared, looking mightily cheery and carrying a box.

"Don't think cakes are going to get you off the hook."

"They're not cakes, they're vegan protein balls. I had to make a small detour in my journey, to retrieve them from my sister's."

"What? Why?"

"I know you're on a health kick, and she makes them."

He placed the box in front of me and I lifted the lid. They looked gorgeous. I pulled one out and nibbled on it. Confectionary heaven. My nibbling changed to devouring and ball number one was gone in seconds.

"D..n't th..; …"

I thought better of my speech and swallowed before continuing.

"Don't think this lets you off if you're late again."

"I wouldn't dream of it, my darling … Cassandra."

Quill sat down and crossed one sartorial leg over the other. This was a three-piece suit and silk tie type of day.

"What's on the calendar? I seem to remember you saying something about a trip to visit a Laird."

That explained the clothing choices. He was going to be sorely disappointed when he realized he wasn't part of the deal.

"I'm going alone. No room on the bike. Sorry."

His eyebrows drew together in a look I had fast come to realise, meant trouble.

"You need me."

"I can assure you, I don't."

"You do."

His persistence got my Scottish dander up. My dander would be right up his bahookie soon if he didn't stop arguing with me. The definitions of both boss and employee seemed to escape him.

Before I had a chance to explode, he continued, "You also need my mate, Vinnie the Knife."

This took it to new heights even for the exotic Quill. Surely there were no ties to the Mafia in his past. Containing my urge to fire him on the spot, I decided to explore further. I sneakily felt like a real PI at last.

"Vinnie the Knife. Where's he from, the Bronx?"

An upturned eyebrow served as an exclamation mark.

"Nah, Whitfield."

"Who, in Whitfield, would saddle their kid with a moniker like Vinnie?" Astonishment radiated from every syllable. "They'd kill him at school."

"His real name's Joe Smith. He thinks he's a hard boy and he carries. A knife that is, not a gun. Gave himself the name."

He pulled an imaginary knife from his pocket and brandished it in my direction.

With a quick parry and sidestep I said, "No hard boys waving knives. In fact, no one waving a knife. We're keeping this legit."

I just about held a falsetto squeak at bay. All these shenanigans were going to turn me into a permanent soprano.

"Vinnie's five foot four and lugs twenty-four stone. Nothing hard about him. More like the Pillsbury Doughboy. He's not long out of the Nick and looking for a job. He'll act as a distraction."

"Aint happening. Besides we've no transport."

"I'm telling you, you need backup. Besides he's got a car and he likes dogs. He could walk Eagal round the grounds and scout things out."

The bone-idle mutt didn't even have the energy to cock an ear at mention of his name.

I chewed on my lip. If nothing else the shaggy rug would get a long walk. If the ancestral pile was like any other in Scotland it would have grounds bigger than some shires. Giving in into the inevitable I picked up the phone. "What's his number? No knives, though. That's non-negotiable."

"Anything you say, Cassandra. Your wish is my command."

Yeh, right. My wish was his to decide whether it would happen or not. I bet he ruled Perth Prison when he was inside. To stay as boss of this Investigator gig I needed to improve at ordering the staff around. Talking of staff, I needed granddad to man the phones.

20

Grandad couldn't oblige. He was on chauffeur duty taking my grandmother and her cronies on a day trip. I could just imagine his joy. The hapless Angus, my usual next step, would be in the middle of completely changing the layout of my flat. If he'd managed to get up from my sofa that is. This left the answering machine. Not ideal, but this one was top of the range and cost as much as your average car. I set it, or at least I think I did, and arranged to meet Quill and Vinnie at a tea shop just outside the castle. We'd reconnoitre there.

Reconnoitre, in PI speak, means tea and sticky buns. I had black coffee and another protein ball. Coconut and macadamia if anyone is wondering. The other pair ate half their body weight in sugar. The rake-like, Quill must have a phenomenal metabolism. Eagal spirited three cakes off the plate before we could stop him. One swallow and they were gone. The only bonus to this was he'd lead my pair of helpers a merry dance and hopefully wear himself out.

Our strategy - I'd shimmy on up to the front door and ask for Lady Lucy. The others would take a stroll around the perimeter of the castle.

"You haven't brought any weapons, have you?" I stared sternly at Vinnie. At least I hoped it was sternly. I've not quite mastered the art as yet, despite practising my Holmes impression in front of the bathroom mirror.

"Nae chance. They said if I carried any mair I'd get put away for ten years next time. My ma's no' well and says I've tae stay out of trouble."

"Your mum's a wise lady. You'd best mind her and look out for her health."

"Aye."

Thank heavens Vinnie aimed for brevity. It made a refreshing change.

My transformation to chic woman of the world had taken place in the confines, and I mean confines, of the café loo. I now had a bruise the size of Aberdeen on my elbow. Concealer had worked wonders with my black eye. I was ready to take on the Laird and all assorted hangers-on. Not that he must have many hangers-on these days. It's rumoured the aristocracy are as poor as church mice.

How wrong could one PI be? This member of the aristocracy had an old-fashioned butler. I mean, how many of those are kicking around these days? He looked at me like I'd killed his favourite grandkid and snatched the business card from my hands. After studying it for more seconds than was comfortable he ushered me through the ginormous wooden doors and into a room.

A stern voice told me to wait. "Lady Lamont will be with you in a moment."

"Thanks."

"Don't touch anything."

He tottered off shutting the door firmly behind him.

My prison was the fanciest room I'd ever had the privilege to set foot in. Remember this is from someone who hobnobbed with the nobs during her stint at the Royal Ballet. It had a fireplace you could roast Goliath in, never mind a suckling pig. That will give you an idea of the sheer scale. I wandered about, eyeing up the chandelier that hung from the painted ceiling. If it came crashing down they wouldn't find my remains until Christmas. That's how long it would take them to clean up.

Don't touch, he'd said. Not a chance. I was frightened to even glance at anything. I'd be paying off the debt for the rest of my natural.

I contemplated whether they'd employed Michelangelo to paint the ceiling when the door opened, and Lady Lucy came gliding in. Even wearing jeans, she was head to toe designer elegance. Yves St Laurent, no less. I thanked my lucky stars and my sainted mother for the fact I sported a Giorgio Armani skirt. She can be a right snob at times. My mother, not Giorgio. Some of it rubbed off on me.

For a fleeting moment I thought about what my suited and booted sidekick was doing. Then shoved it from my mind. Best not to think too hard. Or even think at all. Not with Quill involved.

I didn't even want to start on the knife-toting, heavyweight mate he spent time with. I shuddered, the only natural progression from my train of thought.

Lady Lucy was both charming and welcoming.

"Please sit down. Would you like a drink?"

Jeeves, or whatever his name was materialized at her side.

"Coffee please, Simmons."

A rhetorical question then. Looked like I was having coffee. At the rate I consumed coffee I'd be swinging from the chandelier not being buried by it. This made me giggle. I tried to suppress it. The look in my client's eye stopped it in its tracks. Her look said I'm about to fire this halfwit.

Quite frankly, I wouldn't blame her.

"I take it that this visit means you have found Theo's teddy?"

Not the brightest candle in the chandelier. Did I look like I was clutching a teddy?

"Not as yet, but I am following a few leads."

Truth-stretching was becoming rather natural to me, as the only lead being followed was Eagal's. You know how well that's going.

"Theo can't sleep without it. The nanny keeps bringing him to my room. I can't take much more."

Come to mention it she did look a tad heavy under the eyes. Covert staring elicited the fact she had a shiner bigger than mine. She was better with the concealer than me. I needed a professional make-up artist to do mine. Interesting.

"You seem rather interested in my face."

Not as covert as I thought. Rats. I needed to get better at this investigating lark. I was in serious danger of alienating my most important client. Wondering if being sacked meant I needed to give the money back, I dragged my mind over the contract. Nah. There was a clause in about the dosh being mine, whatever. Thank God for good old Uncle Will's business savvy.

Fortunately, a maid appeared with a tea trolley, saving me from making a prat of myself with an answer. I have to say, in ripped jeans and a top that left little to the imagination she didn't fit my idea of a maid. She looked about sixteen. Maybe they were harder up for help than I thought.

Those thoughts took a more prosaic turn as I eyed up the sugary confections. They battled against maintaining my slim figure and feeding my always present sugar addiction.

Bone china plates, each one of which probably cost more than my annual pay at the Royal Ballet, groaned with cakes. Eclairs, meringues, strawberry tarts and vanilla slices vied for attention. They were eclipsed by a huge chocolate cake, smothered in flowers made with dark and white chocolate fondant.

I wondered if cook would like to move to Dundee and live with me. She and my mother would be able to talk confectionary heaven the whole day long.

I felt like I'd died and gone to heaven.

"Fenella, why are you doing the maid's job for her?"

Lucy turned towards me. "Meet my stepdaughter. She appears to be doubling as the hired help."

"Maid's sick. So, cook asked me to bring this in. I'm nothing but a skivvy."

Whilst this enlightening conversation took place I busied myself with demolishing a chocolate éclair. Sugar addiction had won the duel.

After the last swallow, I said, "Would it be possible for me to speak to you Fenella. I'm trying to find your brother's missing teddy."

"Fine. Anything to shut the snivelling little brat up. I'll be in my room."

She turned abruptly on her heel, inserting earbuds as she went.

"Fenella Lamont, you will be grounded for a year."

Lucy's strident tones must have penetrated whatever music was attempting to drown out the adults.

"Whatever."

A slammed door ended the conversation for good. Or at least until I caught up with her. She wasn't getting off without an interrogation, brat or otherwise. I shoved my natural instinct to be nice to anyone under the age of eighteen, right to one side. A PI coddles no one in the search for the truth.

21

We sat in stunned silence for a few minutes. I didn't like to say anything and by the look of Lucy's face, I'd say she was attempting to bring her emotions under control. She wasn't making much of a fist of it.

"That girl will be the death of me."

I could tell she meant she'd rather see her stepdaughter dead. Even her cultured tones couldn't hide the hatred. Not all sweetness and light in the Lamont household then. A stately home did not a united family make.

Her hands shook as she poured coffee into bone china tea cups. Anyone dropping one of those cups would soon find themselves in a debt so deep they'd never dig themselves out.

While I tried to manoeuvre the minuscule handle, I speculated as to why she was so nervous? Surely a skirmish with a teen wouldn't have her this worked up.

I took my time chewing some lemon shortbread so light it crumbled, melted and danced a tango on my tongue.

It gave her a couple of minutes to recover from whatever was making her skittish.

"I need to speak to members of your household."

She looked sceptical but said, "Of course."

"And your husband?"

"Please leave him out of this." Her tone, though mild, was tinged with steel.

"It would really be—"

"I employ you. There is no need to worry Roderic."

I thought there was every need to worry Roderic, but it wasn't worth arguing the toss with her. I'd still chat to her husband. A husband too free with his fists, if her keeker was anything to go by.

I considered the plate of cakes and wondered if my balletic figure could handle another. I decided against it on a number of fronts. One would assume that slimness and agility might be an advantage in the PI world.

"Has anything come to light since we last spoke?" I remembered the time is money adage. Moving her along was in both of our interests.

"Not to my knowledge."

Interesting choice of answer. I'd bet her cheque on their being more to this than met her Gucci sunspecs.

"Look, if you want me to find your flaming teddy you need to start being straight with me. What do you know."

My Russian temper was never far from the surface.

Her face said I was going the way of the missing teddy. Her voice remained mild.

"May I remind you, I am your employer. There may be someone who knows Bart's whereabouts, but it is not me. Now you mentioned you wanted to speak to my staff."

Before I could reply the door opened and Quill marched in. Accompanied by what I could only describe as a minder. He had to stoop to reach Quill's collar and had muscles a gold medal weightlifter would envy.

Quill struggled as he said, "Kindly remove your hands from my person. I will be alerting the police of this assault." He accompanied this by a swift kick at the man's shins. Actions and words in one seamless pas de deux.

Minder yelled. A bit OTT for a pair of loafers from a dwarf. I wondered if they had steel toecaps.

Then my blood curdled as I realised they probably did.

"You're the guy who was trespassing, dude."

One meaty fist picked Quill up and shook him.

Quill responded by punching at Minder's arm, or rather thin air. His fists couldn't reach. I swear he growled. Either that or muttering obscenities and didn't want us ladies to hear.

"Clint, how dare you interrupt me."

"This jerk says he's with her, Ma'am."

He indicated me with a twitch of his chin. His Texan drawl begged for a Stetson and a pair of Oakley's.

"Sir, I can assure you I am legitimate. Now, please unhand me and let these dear ladies get on with their meeting."

Lucinda tossed him a fond look. Her gaze, when it landed on Clint, was far from fond.

"Let the gentleman go, and you can leave."

"But, Ma'am—"

"Clint, did I not make myself clear."

Minder dropped Quill, who responded by head-butting him in parts further south than is normal when performing such maneouvres. Clint clutched his nether regions with one hand and swung at my helper with the other. Quill ducked under his arm and made a bolt for it, Clint in hot pursuit. This being an unfair contest Minder caught up too quickly. In a counter move, Quill ducked down and scampered through his legs. Clint's next parry resulted in him crashing into a table. Cloisonné if I'm not mistaken. Yes, I had been boning up on all things antique.

We all froze as a vase teetered, looked like it would right itself, quickly changed its mind and hurled itself at the floor. At warp speed. Pieces scattered far and wide.

After two minutes of frozen silence, as though in remembrance of the deceased vase, Lucinda said, "Clint, get out of my sight."

"But—"

"Now." Her tone brooked no arguments.

He left with a look that could curdle lemonade.

Quill sidled up to Lady Lucy and set out to charm her. It took precisely 2.87 seconds before she became putty in his hands. My Lothario assistant had done it again. By this point, I was in awe of his abilities.

"Please, do join us Mr…?"

"Quilleran, my dear. I'm Quill to my friends."

I wondered whether to leave this lovefest and let Quill interview her. The fact he was still on probation, both criminally and in my agency, changed my mind. I wasn't in the mood for explaining my employee's previous career to anyone. Certainly not my best paying client.

"I'm so sorry about the vase." I threw Quill a 'your fired' look. "And about the attack on your staff member."

"You've done me a favour. I'm not sure who or what I hate most, Clint or the vase." She burst out laughing.

"You lot can come again. Best laugh I've 'ad in ages."

The posh accent had slipped somewhat. Seems Lady Lucy came from a lower class of background than she portrayed. Cockney by the sounds of it. Cracking actress though to keep that accent up.

Was she an actress? Maybe I'd have to look into her background. And Roderic's. It struck me that maybe I should have done this days ago. Some detective I was turning out to be.

22

No amount of questioning got any more info from my client. Posh Lady Lucy was back in evidence. She politely enquired if I needed more money. I thought about saying yes, but honesty got the better of me. A rep for fleecing my clients wouldn't look good. If I ever solved this case I wanted word of mouth referrals. A better look for boosting the coffers.

I left her to the tender mercies of Quill. I was sure he would charm the intelligence from her and leave with a Ming Dynasty plate tucked under his arm. Legally. I'd have to search his pockets for anything illegal.

I took a leisurely stroll to Fenella's room, surprised not to be escorted. This gave me ample opportunity to peer into various other rooms. Gently opening one door I surreptitiously glanced in. Empty. I wandered further in. The square footage might just be larger than Dundee's Caird Hall. Okay, an exaggeration, but it came damn well close. It took my breath away. A four-poster bed and elegant drapes were two of the many expensive features.

A mixture of antique and modern it was the type of house that would be featured in Lifestyles of the Rich and Famous. This left me wondering where all the dosh came from. Castles and penury seemed to be the usual state of affairs. Not in this joint.

Lady Lucy's taste was exquisite. Either that or she'd hired Anouska Anquetil as her interior designer. I scoped out a few other rooms, all elegant. Two of the rooms had different doors and were locked. Triple locked by the looks of things. Somewhat excessive. Unless they were gun rooms. Probably not. I'm not big on the geography of castles, but you would think gun rooms would be in the basement. I vowed to solve the mystery of the locked doors.

Fenella's large bedroom was decorated much like any other teenager's. I thought of the state of our childhood bedrooms which looked like the noonday gun had gone off inside them. This one seemed fairly tidy. Evidence that the castle employed a maid. Or several.

Posters of pop stars I'd never heard of adorned the walls. Trophy's and rosettes told the world she excelled at something. My detective brain said horse riding. I was almost right.

"Dressage," she said in answer to my question.

I reevaluated my opinion of her. The scruff in front of me scrubbed up well. It turned out her horse, Bright Flame the Third, was a Dutch Warmblood. Meant nothing to me, but by her animation, I'd say I should be impressed. I made suitably excited noises.

The conversation limped on halfheartedly. Talk of my previous career turned it around.

"You're Cassandra Claymore. Really?" Hero worship and reverence shone from her baby blues. Not that they were blue, but I liked the phrase.

She'd seen me dance the role of Giselle at the Palais Garnier.

"This is seriously the best moment of my entire life. Wait till I tell my friends I've met Cassandra Claymore."

Who would've thunk my old career would be a great big fat bonus in my new one?

"Can I take a selfie with you?" the teen asked, excitement still filling her voice with awe and wonder.

We arranged ourselves in a suitable pose, her with pouty lips, and several snaps were taken. Her fingers trembled with the effort of abstaining from social media until I'd gone. It's a tough gig being a teenager these days.

I managed to steer the talk in the direction of her brother and the Teddy. Turned out she was fonder of the rug rat than she let on to her stepmother.

"Not much love lost between the two of you?"

"She's okay. I don't want her thinking she's got the upper hand." A grin lit up her beautiful hazel eyes. Flecks of gold danced in the sunlight pouring through the large bay window.

"So, what about this teddy? What's your take on its disappearance?"

"That teddy disappears more often than a junkie to rehab. No one would've noticed if it wasn't for Theo."

"I've heard he's fond of it."

"Fond? He's obsessed. God only knows why. It's been sewn up so many times its more thread than bear. Been in the family for about a thousand years."

"Ever been yours?"

She shuddered theatrically. "Do you know how many brats have sucked on Bart's ears?"

I took it the answer was no. Fastidious type, so I don't think its disappearance was anything to do with her. Unless she'd chucked it in the bin. Why would I be told to back off in that case? Still!

She assured me she hadn't chucked it. She wouldn't even touch it to give it back to her brother. More than fastidious. A touch of OCD. I mentally dropped her from my enquiries. Except as a witness. She was still on that list. Whether she was still on Santa's list could be debated. Not the way she treated poor Lady Lucy. She might find herself deficient a few presents under the tree come Christmas morning.

Deciding to leave, I took one step forward when the door exploded open.

Eagal hurtled through dragging a dishevelled Vinnie in his wake. He launched himself at me before I could take preventative action, resulting in a crash which was less balletic ability and more failed amateur.

Vinnie, unable to halt his rapid forward momentum, collapsed on top of the mutt.

Through a mouthful of dog hair, I heard Fenella say, "Who's this handsome boy?"

Eagal, at the sound of a new voice, threw Vinnie off and charged towards it.

I felt all my limbs, clambered to my feet and ran my hands through my hair. All seemed to be well. I tested my knee. A slight twinge. Nothing out of the ordinary.

The fur covered terrorist and the teenager were fast becoming BFFs.

"Would you like to keep him?"

At this point, I meant what I said. I'd take my chances with my dad over this fiasco every five minutes.

"Can't. Theo's allergic. 'Sides, you'd miss him."

She ruffled Eagal's coat.

"She would, wouldn't she. Yes, she would. Lovely boy like you."

Eagal responded in the only way he knew how, by washing her face. She giggled. A normal teenager after all.

I turned my attention away from this love fest to Vinnie the Knife. Not such a hard boy now. He still lay on the floor groaning.

"You all right."

"My arm's broken."

"I hope it's your knife pulling one."

"That dog's dangerous. Should be put down."

"I'll have you put down if you don't quit moaning. There's nothing wrong with you. Get up."

I deduced from his frantic arm waving neither of them was broken.

He lurched to his feet. Somewhat gingerly. His doughboy physique had served as protection. Whingeing Willy was still in one piece.

I couldn't help wondering how many antiques the blasted animal had broken on his way to find me. In my brain, pounds disappeared from my bank account faster than Eagal on speed.

"Did you pair break anything?"

"My ankle."

"For heaven's sake. I wish you'd broken your jaw, we'd all get some peace.

I was now approaching the 'chuck myself off the parapet' stage of my career.

Instead, I chucked the dog and Vinnie out of the castle.

"Walk him, and do not appear inside these hallowed walls again."

When they trooped off I was somewhat surprised. I don't know who looked more hangdog.

"What a nice man. Great with your dog."

I rethought my initial opinion of young Fenella. Not a girl with discerning taste in men.

"He's a crook."
With that, I stomped off.

23

We reconnoitred back at the office. Vinnie, stuffing himself with a 12-inch cheese, turkey and ham baguette, had cheered right up. This being his only payment for his labours, meant he'd requested a huge slice of cheesecake and a custard doughnut as well. And, inexplicably, a diet coke. Why bother? Quill's mates are the strangest people I've ever had the misfortune to trip over.

I handed over the cash without a murmur. Besides this came under the remit of reasonable expenses. Or so my brain told me. Thanks, Lucinda.

"What's the skinny?" I felt my skills with PI speak were improving.

"Your dog's no' skinny."

I glared at Vinnie. "You're one to speak. Shouldn't you be shimmying off home."

"Nah. I've time yet."

I shook my head.

"Unless you've anything helpful to contribute, keep schtum."

"I'm brighter than I look."

My look said the likelihood of this was zero. Even I didn't know what I was doing, and I'd been genning up on all things investigation. I'm sure reading classic detective novels can be classed as research in my line of work. It can, can't it?

"Leaving my weight challenged pooch aside for the minute, is there anything to report."

"Cassandra there is always something to report."

Despite his run-in with a three-hundred-pound minder, Quill looked as elegant as ever. Every strategically combed hair in place, he wasn't even breaking a sweat. How he managed this in a three-piece woollen suit is anyone's guess. I wondered if he picked this skill up in the slammer.

I shuffled around in my chair before saying, "This report. What is it?"

Quill pulled out a piece of pottery from his pocket. It looked suspiciously like a lump of Ming vase.

It turned out my suspicions were correct. Or almost correct.

Quill stood. "Exhibit A, M'lud."

"Less thespian and more assistant if you please. Your gift for the theatrical is wasting my time and money. Also, thieving antiques, even bits of them, is against the law."

"I'm no antique dealer, but I'd say that's a replica."

"For why?"

He picked up the item in question and pointed to the reign mark. Then, rubbing his thumb over it, he showed me his thumb. Blue ink.

"That mark's fake."

Blowing out my cheeks I sat and thought for a minute. Quill stayed quiet. Both he and Vinnie starred at me. Somewhat disconcerting I must say.

"Either they're broke, or the real McCoy is stored somewhere for safekeeping."

"You want me to find out which? I could interrogate the Laird for you," chipped in Vinnie. "He'll no' be a hard lad with a knife at his throat."

He puffed his chest out in a fine impression of a Bantam Cock. The only difference being this Bantam

Cock was more dangerous.

"Vinnie, dear boy. You know you're posturing. Give it up or Cassandra here will sack you."

I managed to gather my wits and my voice together.

"Sack you. I never employed you." Leaping to my feet I continued, "That's your lot. Out. Now."

I emphasized the seriousness of this statement by assisting him from the chair and accompanying him to the door. The urge to shove him through it strong, I resisted. More for the sake of my back than anything else.

"I could have important information."

"Like what? Vamoose."

He waddled off muttering about life being unfair and he was only trying to help.

I gave him a cheery wave as he left.

"Bring one more of your mates into this business and you'll be roasted in a pit alongside the canine assassin."

"Copy that."

"What?"

"They say it on that programme on the television. The one with the American Navy."

"You're an unpaid detective in a low budget agency in Dundee, not working for Naval intelligence."

"I'm trying to sound good."

"You sound like a prat who doesn't know what he's doing."

A bit like me really.

"Now, leave your mates out of this."

Flaming Nora, the heat was crucifying. I pulled an elastic from my pocket, tugged my hair back and tied it up in a bun. My ballerina past meant I'd been performing this since the day I did my first demi plie. It takes seconds.

"You suit the elegant look."

My assistant really was the charmer. Lost on me though. Too many things to worry about, like faking my way through a couple of investigations.

"Apart from dodgy antiques, any other wisdom to impart?"

"I most certainly do. Pull up a chair."

24

This not only called for a chair but a beverage. Or so Quill told me. Personally, I think he was just spinning it out. He's a bigger chancer than the dog. He certainly eats more. He must have the metabolism of a gazelle as I've seen more fat in a Scottish chippy.

When he started his tale, I was glad we'd fortified ourselves.

"The delightful Mrs McFadyen has a son in prison."

"Who's Mrs McFadyen, and what has her son got to do with missing teddies."

"The Laird's cook, my dear."

His expression said I was a shilling short of a gas meter.

I squirmed around in my seat and wiped sweat from my neck.

Quill took the hint and carried on. "Her son is up to his humongous earlobes in debt. Owes squillions to none other than Liam Laughlin."

I leaned forward, my interest piqued.

The name rang a bell. I sent out a drift net to trawl my memory. It came up trumps.

"The bloke with the Pitbulls?"

"The very one. According to mother dearest, Liam's heavies showed her darling boy the rough treatment then shopped him to the police."

He stopped as a shifty look flitted over his face.

"For various misdemeanors he may, or may not, have carried out."

"So, mummy's not happy and wants him out."

"Bingo, my dear girl. Daily beatings inside until the debt's paid."

The flash of a million-watt light bulb fired my grey cells into action. "It's possible dear Mrs McFadyen, she of the exquisite cakes, might have nicked Bart to sell on?"

"I bow to your superior wisdom, Cassandra."

He hopped off his chair and executed said bow.

"I really wouldn't like to conjecture."

"I wonder exactly how much Bart the Bear is worth?"

Maybe I should have done this long before now. This detecting lark was harder than it looked. I logged into the antiques database, searched, jotted down a few prices, sat back and whistled. I *really* should have done this long before now. I'd have been a lot more diligent in searching out the whereabouts of Bart. No wonder they wanted it back.

"How much?"

Quill was so far on the edge of his seat there was a real danger of him catapulting into the stratosphere. I turned the paper round and he stared.

"A hundred and twenty thousand Euros? For a few scraps of material and some stuffing?"

His voice took on a falsetto quality.

"If I'd known they were worth that much I'd have gone into robbing them myself."

"I think I might have joined you. Seriously, I'm in the wrong profession."

We contemplated this for a few minutes. I inhaled the aroma of my Brazilian blend and took a restorative sip. Quill gazed at his Earl Grey like he was reading leaves and it held the answer to everything. Reality was much more prosaic than my imagining a life of crime.

I sighed and said, "We've left the missing Florian swinging in the wind. See what you can dig up about him from your vast list of shiftless contacts."

He pulled out a diary and picked up the phone.

"You really shouldn't talk about my friends that way, Cassandra."

"Whatever."

I turned to social media, ready to start a search.

Quill's smile lit up the room. There were times when I fully understood why women fell at his feet. I felt a trifle giddy myself.

I'd barely typed the first F before my assistant said, "This answering machine contains a phone message."

I looked up and frowned.

"That blasted machine cost a fortune and I can't even work out when a message is waiting for me."

He handed over the phone. I pressed a few buttons, hummed a lot, pressed more buttons, listened to the message and dropped the phone."

"You're not looking so good, Cassandra."

I felt like I'd had a dodgy curry and it and I were about to part company.

"They... they..." I swallowed hard. "They said, You're a dead woman."

"Did they say anything about offing *me*?"

This shot my dander up higher than Cox's stack, rousing me from my state of terminal shock. Cox was a jute mill and the stack its chimney, so we're talking pretty high here.

"No, they flaming well didn't. Stop worrying about yourself."

I grabbed a crumpled sheet of paper from the desk and chucked it at him. "

Get with the programme. If you've nothing useful to contribute, then keep your trap shut."

"Sorry, but I might..." His voice dropped. "Just might, have a couple of gentlemen looking for me."

This was jaw-dropping stuff if I'd ever heard it.

"What? Why? Wait, why am I hearing about this now?"

I glared at him with as much aggression as I could muster. Not much given the turmoil in my stomach.

"Your interview might have been a good time to fess up."

"I surmise you would not have employed me under those circumstances?"

"You surmise right. I've a good mind to sack you."

The threat was hollow, and he knew it. Still, hostile gangsters were never part of the deal. Now I had Quill's enemies to worry about as well as someone out to kill me.

A thought flashed through my brain. The type that makes the heartbeat flutter and a fog descend inside the skull.

"They wouldn't happen to be mob, would they?"

"My dear Cassandra, your flair for the dramatic is powerful. This is Dundee, not Sicily."

I wondered whether I should mention this turn of events to Lachie. Before or after I lamped Quill. The thought was dismissed quicker than it arrived.

"Nothing would surprise me where you are blasted well concerned. What do these thugs look like?"

I thought I'd better be on the lookout. If they approached me they'd soon find out I could run nearly as well as I could dance. Helps to keep the muscles trim and the weight down.

The descriptions were brief and muddled. It turned out Quill had a vague idea of what they looked like but no clear vision.

From a couple of brief encounters and near misses, he informed me he had channelled his inner Sherlock and deduced, "One has blonde hair, a beard, and a broken nose"

This was not instilling me with confidence.

I tuned back in to his voice.

"The other's bald, batters his head off most shop doors, and wears a facial scar with pride. They both wear suits." He paused, then said, "Or they did when I last bumped into them."

Glory be, this agency was turning into a hotbed of sin, although not quite debauchery. Yet.

"And this would be when?" My calm voice surprised even me.

"Yesterday. In the Scott Café. I extricated myself from the situation by bolting through the back door."

Not good. That café lay just a few meagre streets away. "Exactly how do you know they are looking for you?"

"Nutjob Norm sent me a message saying there was a price on my head."

"Who? This is ridiculous. Why is Norm after you?"

"He's not. He owes me a favour so he gave me the heads up."

"Why on earth does Norm owe you a favour? If he's as much a lunatic as you say, surely you'd be the one owing him favours."

"Better not to ask, Darling."

I put *my* head in my hands. What on earth had I got myself in to?

I sternly told my brain to remind me to phone Lexi. Her underhand dealing had landed me in so much hot water I could take a bath. She more than owed me and I intended to get my revenge in full.

Talking of Lexi, she'd been suspiciously absent since she landed an assistant on my doorstep. She knew a lot more about Quill's shenanigans than she was letting on. I could smell it. Who needs friends like that?

"So where do we go from here?" I said.

"It's elementary."

My eyes rolled so high I felt dizzy.

"What's elementary? Enlighten me."

"Quite honestly, I've no clue, but I was channelling my inner Sherlock."

"Channel your inner Dundee, not Victorian London."

"I think even the wonderful Sherlock and John would have found this case tricky."

"Tricky? I'd say it's nigh well impossible with you being chased by the Dundee mob. Let's solve these blasted cases."

Then I banged the desk with my fist, adding for good measure, "And sort out the goons who're chasing you. I can't take much more of this."

I felt like I should be adding something else. Something more forceful. Any self-respecting PI didn't stand for any nonsense. Not from anyone, and certainly not from employees.

"You're going to get us all killed. Your mobster mates are more likely to come after me than you."

"Cassandra, you must watch your blood pressure. Such a delightful lady as yourself should remain calm. Do you realise the statistics for death by heart attack are higher than by murder? "

I half rose from my chair, prepared to throttle him. Then slumped back down. Doing time for murder wouldn't do much for my reputation.

My reputation was about all I had left. Plus, mamah would really lose bragging rights with a daughter in chokey. Probably the only thing worse than being a PI.

25

Deciding the best way to solve a case was to actually work on it, we bent our heads and ploughed on. I in silence. Quill, on the other hand, made enough noise to wake the dead. His bonhomie and effusive greetings on the phone were getting on my last nerve. I plugged in some eye-wateringly expensive headphones, noise cancelling of course, and plonked them on my head. Within seconds the sound of Tchaikovsky's Dance of the Sugarplum Fairy soothed my zinging nerves. Bliss.

Searching social media, I found Florian used both Facebook and Twitter. I decided a bit of breaking and entering might be in order. Florian being the dumbest bloke in Scotland, even I worked out his password in about eight seconds. His name netted no results, but I hit the jackpot with Mimosa. Who used their sister's name as a password. Gormless doesn't begin to cover it.

Trawling his friends and followers could be classed as an occupational hazard. Mimosa's cheque wasn't large enough for the amount of mindless crap I waded through. Some of it as well as being mindless, bordered on pornographic. I'm surprised the social media algorithms hadn't jumped in and chucked him and his mates off.

At the end of an hour, I was no further forward than when I started. An hour of my life I would never see

I felt a momentary pang of guilt over the fact I was

there illegally. If memory served me right I could be charged with hacking. The size of my paycheque, and the fact that ethical hacking wasn't a crime, brought me some measure of comfort. How the ethical hacking standpoint would hold up in court is another matter. Maybe I should discuss it with Lachie. On second thoughts...

Overall, his social media posts were a load of old tosh. He, and his friends, did a lot of drinking. Period. They seemed to have little else to fill up their days. Except jet off on exotic holidays. My initial thought, he'd jetted off with a girlfriend, was probably spot on. Except for one small fact. Florian usually documented every step of his journey right down to the particular brand of pretzels they served him on the plane. This time it was remarkably quiet. I pondered the fact.

A loud crash penetrated the music and shocked me out of my reverie. Leaping up I ran around the desk. Quill lay on the floor his face covered in slobber.

Deep in thought, I hadn't seen or heard the hellhound mount a stealth attack. The stupid mutt had decided it was playtime. Why he'd focussed on the unsuspecting Quill only Eagal's microscopic brain could answer. I suspect it had something to do with the fact the stupid mutt now thought they were BFFs.

I rushed over and pulled Quill upright. My pooch didn't like the idea of this at all. He immediately launched a frontal attack. A quick counter move and I managed to grab his collar, resulting in me hurtling across the floor carried along by his forward momentum. Quill went flying again and I landed in an ungainly heap beside him. This satisfied the idiotic beast, who slunk back behind the desk.

"You are totally going on tomorrow's barbecue." I pulled my tangled hair from my mouth, stood and brushed myself down.

Quill followed suit, pulled his chair upright and straightened his waistcoat. I thanked my lucky stars it was still in one piece. The chair that is. I had better things to worry me than Quill's waistcoat. My furniture budget currently stood at nil.

"Your canine companion is quite something. He may need Dog training classes." My polite assistant adjusted his tie, ran a hand through his perfectly coiffed hair and clambered up on the seat again.

My thoughts tended towards the 'perhaps I should have him put down' variety. The dog that is, not Quill. I still optimistically thought he would come in useful. Both the dog and Quill this time.

"Been there. Done that. Got the scars." I too sat down and checked myself for injury. I'd got off Scot free. I wasn't sure about Quill but, at the moment, I didn't care.

"They threw him out of obedience school. Couldn't cope with the sheer number of legal threats from the other dog owners."

Quill nodded. A wry curl of a moustached lip indicated he understood. "I have a friend—"

"There's enough of your friends cluttering the place up already. Plus, I don't want the animal chucked off a cliff by one of *your* animals." I glowered in a threatening manner.

"Who said anything about chucking him off a cliff. I have a friend who trains dogs. He may take him on."

"Yeh. Right. How does he train them? Using guns?"

"You are rather hasty in seeing the worst in people,

Cassandra."

Do you blame me? Your friends all seem to have extra names that indicate their state of unfitness for joining normal society. Nutjob Norm, Maniac Mike, Hit Man Horace, Butcher Bob, blah, blah, blah."

"You're making most of those up. You really should go into writing fiction, Dear Lady."

"And you should stop dumping your friends on me as hired help."

At that point, Quill gave up.

26

"What you got for me?" I asked.

I'd spent enough of my precious time on the dog from hell and Quill's cronies. Dear departed Uncle Will didn't have to cope with this, as Eagal was a wee sook when he was around. This meant he spent his time detecting, and not running around after a demented pooch. He made gazillions more than me. Which he promptly squandered on a roulette wheel at the casino, the reason I inherited the agency and not a drachma to go with it. Mamah considered him the black sheep of the family. My father considered him eccentric. I considered him a maniac with a penchant for persecuting any waif or stray who came in his line of sight. The stray being me. What he definitely was, however, was an ace at this private detecting malarkey. Which is more than anyone will ever say about me.

Quill's contacts had netted zilch. Well, slightly more than zilch but as good as. It's impossible to keep a secret in Dundee as someone will usually fess up at the first hint of a stern word. It might be the murder capital of Scotland, but the population are a right bunch of feardies. However, this time it was different."

"Some rather unsavoury characters seem to be well acquainted with our Florian." He stopped.

"And?" I wish he'd just spit things out and forget the dramatic pauses.

"No amount of cajoling or threatening elicited any further details my dear."

"For heaven's sake. What's the point of employing an ex-con if they can't get the dirty on our clients?"

"Much as I would love to help you, my dear lady, the case is a hopeless one."

"Call me, dear lady once more, and your case will also be hopeless. As well as being an ex-con you'll be an ex-PI. A dead one."

Quill, ever the diplomat, moved on. "Did you uncover anything of interest?"

"Likes flash cars. Lives beyond his means. Not a dicky bird out on social media for five days."

"Unusual?"

"You can bet Eagal it is. His life's an open book. I could tell you what he's done for the last six months. Down to what underwear he had on."

"TMI, dear... Cassandra."

"It turns out he does have a girlfriend. A leggy blonde called Kate Smith."

"What do we know about Miss Smith."

From her social media updates, I'd say she got into the gene pool whilst the lifeguard was off duty."

"Bit dim then?"

"And some."

I opened my drawer and pulled out my handbag.

"I'm off to pay Kate a visit."

I thought I'd better take the mutt with me. There being a high chance of him eating my assistant during my absence.

"Eagal. Come."

The shaggy dope opened one eye and closed it again. He let out a little snore for added effect. All the exertions with Quill had worn him out. I grabbed his lead, clipped it on and yanked hard. He rolled over. After a couple more tugs I gave up and resorted to bribery.

At the very sniff of a treat, the mutt leapt to his feet and shook himself. I dodged low flying drool, handed him his treat, and headed for the door.

"Would you like me to accompany you. I could act as a lookout." Quill looked eager.

I contemplated this. Might be a good idea given there were goons out to get him. He would at least be protected. On seconds thought, I couldn't protect a dead gerbil far less an assistant. I decided against it. He was more likely to *attract* trouble than repel it.

"Nah. Stay here and keep looking for Florian. Try not to turn the place into a gangster's hangout while I'm gone."

"You do me a disservice. I told you, I'm a new man. Completely reformed."

"In that case, how come your ex-con mates are still cluttering up your life."

I took one step, then added, "And my life. Keep out of trouble if that's possible."

"I do seem to attract trouble in a way that appears excessive. I swear on my little one's life I am attempting to turn my life around.

"Looks like you've turned it around approximately 360 degrees and are back where you started."

"It would appear to be the case."

"Just do your job. I'll be back before you know it and I want results on my desk on my return.

Quill shook his head and then picked up the phone. I headed out the door and was dragged down the stairs by a now eager dog.

I heard Quill say, "Norm, I've a wee favour... Yep, I'll owe you one after this... Jolly decent of you..."

I groaned. Now Nutjob was right in the middle of my case. *Lexi. you're so dead when I see you.*

27

Sweat trickled down my forehead stinging my eyes on its way to my cheeks. A quick back of hand swipe and they were gone. More followed. Keeping it under control was a pointless act. Once again, I cursed my four-legged companion. Without him, I'd be speeding along to the thrum of a motorbike engine and through a cooling breeze. Or walking at a more sedate pace. Then I felt guilty and ruffled his fur. He responded by licking my hand. It was difficult to hate him for too long.

Cracked paving stones radiated a shimmering heat so strong they could almost melt the leather soles of my sandals. The smell of the drains was overpowering. With no rain for weeks and an imminent hosepipe ban, the last thing on anyone's mind was keeping the drains clean. I gagged. Then told myself to get a grip. Real detectives didn't get themselves worked up about such mundane things as smelly drains. I straightened my back and marched on.

Regret hung like a yoke around my shoulders. Regret that I hadn't waited until later. Something else to add to my endless list of 'should know' in the life of a Dundee detective. I wondered if Eagal's paws were burning, but he seemed to be bounding along happily enough.

Kate lived in a flat off the Perth Road. The bottom end. Just past the University Buildings. The top end would necessitate a bus. The road in question is several miles long and heat exhaustion tends to limit investigative efforts. How was one girl meant to remember so much?

Kate lived up a closie. This is Dundonian for a communal area in the old grey stone tenements. It has endured through the generations. I tied Eagal to a nearby drainpipe. His lead reached to the shade of the closie where he flopped down. I slugged some water from a huge bottle and poured much of the remainder in Eagal's mouth. He lapped it up like a Bedouin at an oasis. The rest I poured over his coat. I'd had enough nonce and foresight to take him for a haircut. Fur coats and a heatwave do not happy bed partners make.

Walking up the cracked stairs I kept well away from the puddles. As it hadn't rained for several weeks I did not want to think about what liquid formed them. I rang the doorbell attached to a scuffed front door. Nothing. I tried again, several times. Maybe it was broken. Hammering on the door elicited no response. Damn. I resorted to that tried and tested method of investigating. I peered through the letterbox. What the…? I staggered back and whipped out my phone. Hands shaking, I misdialled. Tried again 9…9…9. It was answered.
    "Police Scotland."
    "I think someone's dead." I rattled off the address.

Having done my duty, a mist descended in my skull. The sort that makes you want to topple over and land with a thump on the ground. Leaning back against the wall didn't help. Despite the general squalor of the close remaining upright was not an option. I slid down the wall and sat with my knees up to my chin. This brought me closer to the smell of ammonia. The stuff smelling salts are made of. My senses returned quick sharp and I bolted to my feet. I now had a new-found sense of appreciation for those Victorian heroines.

The police arrived within 10 minutes. Took them long enough. You could walk to Perth Road from Bell Street in less time. Must have taken them a few minutes to start the air conditioning or something. Bunch of pansies.

The first one up the stairs? Lachie. Damn. The last thing I needed was him on my case spouting overwhelming amounts of brotherly scorn.

"Out of the way, Brat."

"Charming."

"I'm working." His tone was terse.

He carried a lethal looking battering ram and wasted no time in putting it to good use. Even I admired his expertise. Maybe I should keep on his good side in future.

No sooner had the door flown open than a brace of paramedics flew up the stairs and charged into the flat. I followed, wanting a front row seat. Dead body or not.

It turned out my 'corpse' was very much alive. Thank God. I know PI's come across some unsavoury sights on a regular basis, but I did not relish this part of my role. Alive and conscious in the opinion of the dishy paramedic who bent over her. The her being, Kate.

"Drunk as a topper on payday if the smell of her breath is anything to go by," he said.

Giving the paramedics some privacy, I wandered off. Two steps and a yank on my arm stopped me in my tracks.

"Where do you think you're going?" Lachie's raised eyebrow spelled trouble.

"I told you to come and see me this morning. You didn't." I changed the subject.

"First I've heard of it.

"I left a message in your office. With your P.A."

He shook his head. "What P.A.? Police Scotland don't spring to such things."

Another head shake. "Never mind that. What the devil has it got to do with you wandering around this flat?"

Mustering up my best enigmatic stare I gave him time. I was a master at handling my favourite brother. The current favourite as I had high hopes of his job assisting me with mine.

He took a couple of deep breaths. His voice steadier, he said, "Why are you here? What are you doing?"

"You need to keep that temper of yours under control. That's two questions."

My bravado hid the fact my stomach felt decidedly queasy.

He thumped the wall, yelped and sucked his knuckles. "Answer the blasted questions."

"Lachie Claymore get a grip. Mamah would be black affronted if she saw your behaviour."

I glared at him, then said, "I wanted you to do a search for Kate Smith."

"Who's she, and why are you looking for her?"

"And another two questions."

"Cass, I swear…"

"She's the woman lying over there." I pointed to the patient, who was now groaning. Remembering the 'time is money' adage, I succinctly outlined my case omitting any mention of Florian by name. Some cards you needed to keep close to your chest.

"If you'd done what you were meant to do, I wouldn't be here, Lachlan Claymore."

"Who made you the boss of me. Keep out of the freaking way."

I had absolutely no intention of following his orders. He knew it.

"Still, if I hadn't been here she might have died."
"Still dramatic after all those years."

The minute he turned his back I hived off into the bedroom. Neat. Tidy. Heroin paraphernalia on the limed wood bedroom table. Woah. My brain took a few seconds to register this. What?

I backed out of the room and tripped over a passing paramedic.

"You need to have a look in there."

Dishy number two took one look at me and bolted in the direction of my pointing finger. He shot out faster than he went in. "Possible heroin overdose."

They got busy with needles and syringes.

Before they could load her onto a stretcher a furry tornado burst through the door.

Eagal, who had freed himself from his shackles, wanted to party. He trailed a large piece of plastic drainpipe behind him, scattering policemen and paramedics in his wake. He charged up the hallway, or lobby as they say around these parts, towards the still unconscious Kate.

She did not remain unconscious for long. A quick wash from Eagal's tongue had her shoving him away. Or maybe it had more to do with the medication our knights in blue and green shoved in her arm.

I grabbed the canine terrorist's lead and made a hasty escape. I wondered if Florian also lay in a drug-induced coma somewhere. It was clear I wouldn't be interviewing Miss Kate Smith about the matter any time soon. Having got the bit between my teeth, you could bet Bart that I'd be grilling her at some point. I made a note on my phone calendar to remind myself to follow up. Us modern detectives are cutting edge. Notebooks are so yesterday.

Pulp fiction detectives worldwide would be proud of my dogged determination, natural curiosity and ability to muck the whole thing up. Either that or they'd put me down as a crackpot. Or just plain put me down.

28

I'd not even made it a hundred yards down the road before Lachie caught up with me. "D'you want a lift?"

"With the blue light brigade?"

"Duh. We're plain clothes, dummy."

"You're right cutting sometimes. Play nicely."

He raised a quizzical eyebrow. "Lift?"

"Sure." Eagal clambered in the back and I squeezed in beside him.

This left no room for one of the coppers. He said he would walk. Bending down he whispered in my ear, "I'm going to nip to the bookies anyway," and winked as he loped off.

My 'by the book' brother wouldn't like that one. I didn't inform him. Always good to have a stray bobby in your back pocket. Especially if you've no earthly clue what you're doing.

Dumped unceremoniously outside my office, I clattered up the stairs and entered it saying, "You'll never believe…"

I was talking to thin air. "Quill?" No response.

The kitchen was empty, as was the one and only toilet. Equality rules around here. Where the blazes could he be? I swear I gave him specific instructions to stay put and work hard. How had that been translated into take off the minute my back is turned?

I put down some food and water for a nearly comatose Eagal. This revived him enough to scarf and slurp. It's hard work being a doggie terrorist. I brewed myself a nice cup of Darjeeling, the temperature level being more suited to this than Brazilian Blend.

While it brewed I downed a couple of large glasses of water. Crystal glass of course. Being a PI didn't mean I needed to let my prima donna standards slip. I digress. Lachie wouldn't let me drink any in Kate's flat. Something about DNA and evidence. Goodness only knows why, as no crime was committed. Unless using heroin was a crime. Was it? He did let me give Eagal a bowl of water though. His DNA didn't matter. The amount he drooled his DNA would be all over the crime scene like scabies. Only twice as prolific.

I paid homage to the search on Google and soon had my answer. It was an offence against the Misuse of Drugs Act, Possessing a Class A Drug.

A flashbulb went off in my brain. More searching. If someone unknown had forced the heroin on her then it was Administration of a noxious substance, drugging and attempts.

Maybe Florian had drugged her. This raised several more questions, the answering of which I found impossible.

Was Florian holed up with her before he drugged her and scarpered?

Was the disappearance new?

Was he really missing, or avoiding Mimosa?

Actually, I quite liked that version. If I were him I'd do everything I could to avoid the odious bint. I didn't really think this was the answer. He genuinely loved his sister. Or did when we were at school. I can't see that having changed, especially since her bank balance seemed to have eye-watering sums in it. I remember him flashing the cash at school. Daddy was a squillionaire or something but cut Florian off at the pass when he started using the money to develop his career as a drug Lord. The lad seemed to pull himself together after that, and the drug empire never got past the lower level.

All this thinking gave me a headache. I rummaged around in my handbag and found a couple of paracetamol. Opening up my computer I entered the questions in a neat list. If nothing else, it looked efficient and made me feel better. Time to start gathering some answers. I picked up the phone and called the elusive Quill.

"Where in the blue blazes are you?"

"After a hot lead. No time to chat."

I was unceremoniously cut off. At this rate, his probation was going to be short-lived. Either that or I'd be doing time for murder.

I drummed my fingers on the desk. No one to talk to and nowhere else to go. I felt like Billy No Mates. A particularly dense one.

I sighed and gave in to the next unpleasant task. Picking up the phone I dialled Mimosa's number.

"What do you want. Unless you've found him, shove off."

Yet again I wondered if Florian wanted to be found.

"Always a pleasure to talk to you, Mimosa. I'm afraid Florian is still on the lam."

"He's not on the run, he's missing. You never were very bright."

Whatever. This coming from someone who has two brains. Lost one and the other's been out searching ever since.

"Have you any contact details for his mates?"

"Do you think I'm the phone directory. Look it up yourself."

After taking several calming breaths I said, "Their names would be helpful."

She rattled off several likely names before slamming the phone down. I made the assumption re slamming based on listening to the screech of the 'call ended' tone. Mimosa's personality aided the deduction. Sherlock would be proud.

My first call netted a response of, "I'm on night duty you stupid cow. Foxtrot Oscar." For the sake of sensibility, I've substituted this phrase for a stronger expletive. Strike one.

Calls two three and four netted a similar number of strikes. They either hadn't seen him in ages or were looking for him as he'd tapped them for money. Substantial amounts. An image of a wastrel began to emerge.

Strike four was a little more enlightening.

"I'd say he's in the Tay, wearing concrete boots."

Even I was taken aback at this revelation.

"What makes you say that?"

"Pretty obvious you don't know him." The voice roughened. "What you after him for?"

"Private Investigator. His sister's looking for him." I hurried to insert this before his suspicions led to more phone slamming.

"Tell her to leave the country. If he's disappeared they'll be after her next."

It would appear that Mimosa's safety now appeared to be in my hands. How the freak did that happen?

My day was fast becoming short-lived. Much like most of the conversations I'd had. Home time approached. Not like a thief in the night, more like one that came in and battered me over the head with a mallet.

Still, the recalcitrant Quill did not appear. I had a sneaking suspicion whatever he was doing he was trying his hardest to drive me to drink. What I wouldn't give for one right now. This job was turning me into an alky. That's an alcoholic to the rest of you.

I wondered if my mother had any champagne in the house. My favourite tipple. Born in the upmarket wine bars of London. Ballet dancers we might be, but when released from the shackles we knew how to party. My current income stretched to decent wine, Not champagne. The decent stuff. No self-respecting connoisseur would even think about drinking the cheap stuff.

29

I thought I'd head to menopause mansions for a feed. The flush of new clients might have me rattling money in my pocket, but I wasn't keen to spend it on food. Not when I could eat it for free. My thrifty Scottish upbringing.

Mamah also stocked several bags of nosh for the shaggy rug. My dear, departed uncle's generous provision in his will did not run to any money for feeding the canine inheritance. Rather remiss if you ask me. That dog cost more than the entire agency was worth. What's the phrase, a poisoned chalice?

We walked, or rather ran, there. Eagal's jaunt up the Perth Road hadn't done much to suppress his energy levels. A straight route along the waterfront, it was a glorious journey. The bright sunlight sent diamonds of light dancing on the silvery water of the River Tay. Approaching Broughty Ferry the smell of seaweed hung strong in the air, reminding me once more of why I love my native city.

Fat drops of sweat dripping down my face reminded me of the temperature. I stopped at a corner shop so small it would be classed as a cupboard. Much of its stock seemed to be water. Hooray. I bought a couple of bottles and begged the loan of a bowl. We're a nation of animal lovers so a bowl materialized and Eagal was soon rehydrated. Not wanting to push my luck, I drank from the bottle.

When I arrived at the parentals', Eagal shot into the kitchen and flopped on the floor. He managed to look pitiful in his lump of plastic.

"Have you not fed that animal, Cassandra?"

Mamah's clothing choice was somewhat less revealing today. Come to think of it the kitchen seemed much cooler. This might be due to the top of the range air conditioner that now resided in one corner. My father got fed up with her whining about the heat. This overcome his thrifty nature.

The kitchen counters bowed with the weight of food. As always Mamah was cooking enough to feed Broughty Ferry with a large chunk of Barnhill thrown in.

"He's a wee actor. Ignore him. That beast eats better than me."

"What's happened to him?"

"Another door bites the dust."

Mamah nodded and shovelled food into a bowl for him. He fell on it like he'd that minute returned from a diet farm. What a chancer.

"The poor soul's starving."

"The only starving soul around here is me. What's for dinner?"

I grabbed a cracker and some caviar from the counter. A Petrov relative had obviously recently returned from Russia if there was caviar around. It usually meant champagne as well. Hallelujah. I perked right up and bolted for the fridge.

Mamah headed me off at the pass with her next words.

"Your husband's in the kitchen."

Screeching to a halt I entered full height fight 'em off mode. "I. Haven't. Got. A. Husband."

What I had was an ex-husband. In fact, he couldn't be

exer if he tried. I was married to Sergei Sokolov for precisely three weeks, 2 days, 13 hours. That the amount of time it took me to find out he was doing a midnight dance a deux with the Corps de Ballet. The entire Corps de Ballet. Well, almost. He stuck to the ones who were over the age of consent. He charmed them with his Russian Prince routine. They might not be so keen on Harry Copperbottom from a sink estate in Birmingham.

"Stop shouting, missy. No one is deaf in this household."

I ignored her, picked up the nearest weapon and stomped off to find him.

"Cassandra, that's quite enough. You're stealing my wooden spoon."

Interfering with a kitchen implement was a capital offence in our house. I flung it in her general direction, grabbed a bottle of champagne from the fridge and resumed my stomping. A bottle would make a much more satisfying weapon.

"What are you doing in, Dundee?"

He opened his mouth.

"Never mind that, what are you doing in Scotland?"

"Eating haggis with your grandad. They're Bostin'."

"Get out of my country. Now."

Plonking the bottle down on the table, I yanked the back of his chair. A loud crack followed. I stared at the piece of wood in my hand. Mamah was going to freak. So incensed at the sudden appearance of my ex, I didn't care.

Sergei twisted round and took in my astonishment. "Now look what you've done, Cassie. You need to reign in that temper of yours."

Another loud crack was heard as the wood made contact with his head.

"Get out of my universe."

Harry leapt up, rubbing his head.

"What the hell?" Swivelling round he added, "Lachie, arrest her."

My brother shoved another forkful of haggis in his mouth and chewed.

"She assaulted me."

"Sit down and shut up you wuss. She barely tapped you. I'd have smacked you harder." His mouth discharged Haggis like shot from a cannon. A dob hit Sergei in the face. Best laugh I'd had in ages.

Sergei glowered and muttered, "Police brutality." He returned to chewing his haggis.

I contemplated liberating one of my father's antique guns. A blunderbuss would soon put him in his place. Shame there wasn't ammunition to go with any of the guns. Nor could they fire. Damn.

"I'm no' sure why he's here either, hen. He's eating more than his fair share o' our tea."

Stealing food from granddad was not the best move Harry ever made. Elgin took mealtimes seriously.

"How come you're eating here? Gran's cooking not up to scratch?"

Granny Claymore's cooking beat my mum's, and that's saying something.

"She's gone out with her pals. I declined their kind offer to join them. Only so much knitting talk a man can take, now what I mean." He contemplated his plate. "Besides, I kent there was Haggis on the menu at your mum's hoose."

"Poor wee soul." A Scottish platitude, I actually

meant it. Granny could talk about knitting, crochet and sewing long enough to make a strong woman weep. I loved her dearly, but she needed a new hobby.

"Right enough." Granddad returned to eating his tea. Haggis is not a dish best served cold.

The shaggy rug on legs now occupied himself in the garden. Goodness knows what he was chasing, but only he could see it.

I grabbed some vegetarian delights from the kitchen and joined the others. Glaring at Harry, after every few mouthfuls, kept me gainfully occupied.

In the end, I said, "What are you really here for? My mother's cooking's the bizz, but it's not worth a trip from London. You could have gone to Simpson's in the Strand for a feed."

Simpson's, for those of you who have not had the good fortune to eat there, is an upmarket British restaurant. Their barley and cauliflower cheese with a walnut parfait is sublime.

Before the useless lummock could open his mouth, Grandad exploded.

"Whatever you say'll be a load of old Horlicks. You treated my lassie something shocking."

Even I wasn't going to pick grandad up for that one. Besides, I suspected he was toning it down for the women present. He could swear like a dockhand when he wanted to.

"You tell him, Grandad."

Grandad carried on giving it laldy, leaving my ex in no uncertain terms as to his failings in the husband department. It would make a strong man blush.

Any normal man that is. Harry just stared with an inane grin on his face. "You can be fierce when you want to be. I'm here to woo your young lassie back."

I gulped down a whole flute of Zolotaya Balka, a rather nice fizzy from the Crimea. It deserved to be sipped and luxuriated, but Harry's words called for desperate measures. I felt like kicking his woo, right up his woowoo.

"Over my dead body. Or your dead body. It's still debatable which."

I had an overwhelming urge to perform a Grand Jeté catching him right in the consequentials on the upward splits. Cool his ardour right down to zero that would. How come my mother let the odious git stay to tea anyway.

I stood and did more stomping, this time in the direction of the kitchen. I asked her that very question.

"He's your husband, and he says he still loves you."

"Your daughter married to a serial philanderer is more appealing than her being a divorced PI?"

"Don't be so rude, young lady."

"Loves me? Are you having a giraffe?"

"Cassandra, I brought you up properly. Please speak correctly."

Greek scholar, Mamah was out in all her fearsome glory.

"By the way, you'll be needing Angus to mend one of the dining room chairs." The petulant tinge to my voice surprised even me.

"I'll take it to a professional. Angus is far too busy."

Far too busy sleeping. Mum's defence of her youngest son only stretched so far. She loved her antique furniture too much to leave it in Angus's incapable hands.

Having no sane response to any of this I grabbed

Eagal's collar. Nose in the trough once again, he was not keen to depart. Judicious hauling and shouting propelled him out of the kitchen and in the direction of the front door.

Hurtling past the dining room I yelled, "Lachie, come and see me tomorrow."

He looked up from his cherry blini; waved a laconic hand. I wasn't sure if the sign meant fine or no chance. One was never sure with Lachie, so it could also mean I'm coming to arrest you tomorrow. Hopefully, he'd comply this time. With the summons, not the arrest.

Outside, on a still sizzling pavement, I realized I needed transport. Taxi drivers sped up and refused to stop when they took one look at Eagal. My body, now groaning with the weight of Mamah's food, dug its toes in and refused to take one step. I cajoled and encouraged. No joy. The answer was still no. The champagne sloshing around in my belly had the last word. It threatened to reappear if I even thought about a run.

I turned back towards the house. There was nothing for it but to beg one of my numerous offspring for a lift. Granddaddy had been swigging as much bubbly as me so in no fit state to drive. He planned on staying the night. My father had also indulged in a couple of glasses of champagne.

"Come on, you lot. Help a girl out."

My knight in shining armour turned out to be Angus. He hadn't managed to muster up the energy to find himself a can of beer so, was the only one in the household legally fit to drive. Who knew laziness would turn out to be a virtue.

You only had to sniff a barmaid's apron to be over the

limit in Scotland. Quite right too. After being mown down by a drunk driver I have a strong moral code when it comes to drinking and driving.

30

I returned to a voice message.

"There's a surprise package on its way, darling. Yours to keep and do with as you will. You'll love it."

No name, but I recognised the vague tones of my sister, Jacinta. A free spirit, if she were any freer she'd be a spirit for real. She was presently in Bolivia, Columbia, Peru or some such place. South America anyway. I had a feeling I wouldn't like this surprise. Knowing her it would be an Alpaca. A live one. I liked alpaca wool as much as any woman but drew the line at producing my own. Besides Eagal would probably eat the damn animal.

As if he could read my mind the hound from hell sat down by his food bowl and howled. Seriously!

"Not a chance, pal. You've eaten enough to feed Dundee."

He threw me a dirty look.

"Wasted on me."

He slunk off to the bedroom, head hung low. Another night on the sofa for me. I wouldn't mind, but he had a top of the range bed of his own, located in another bedroom. He and I needed to have stern words. My highly toned balletic physique needs a decent night's sleep.

The thought of my sleeping arrangements flew from my mind with the arrival of Larbert. Straight into the sitting room. Without ringing the doorbell.

"Have you had a key cut for this house?" I was determined to solve the mystery of his sudden appearances.

"Nope."

"How the freak do you get in here?"

"I'm a fireman. Doors are easy peasy."

"Didn't involve an axe then?"

"Axes are so yesterday. Come here."

He pulled me into his arms. I shoved him off. I needed to learn this door opening trick. Could come in handy in my line of work. The lack of progress on these cases had me thinking a spot of illegal breaking and entering might be the best idea in the history of my career as a PI

"No kissing until I know how to open doors without keys."

The petulant look on his face would have beaten little Sophia at her best. Big baby. He stood, grabbed my hand and dragged me towards my front door.

It turned out his lock breaking *was* easy peasy and involved a nifty tool. He showed me how to use it. Promised me a set. Something to do with the no kissing rule. After striking the deal, we returned to the arm pulling which led to much more exciting things than breaking locks.

Eventually, I pulled away and brought him up to date on my cases.

"It's an exciting life you lead. Easier being a fireman."

"You allowed to call yourself that now. Isn't it fire person?"

"Officer if you want to be picky. I'm the old-fashioned type."

"You get around in your line of work. Do you know

anything about Florian?"

"What makes you think I know everyone 'ere in Dundee. I'm a Laaandan lad."

"Six degrees of separation falls to about two degrees where Dundee's concerned."

During our witty exchange, I trotted to the kitchen and returned with supplies. Of the liquid kind. Along with a couple of heavy antique crystal wine glasses.

Larbert busied himself pouring two glasses of a crisp Sancerre. Straight from the fridge, it cooled the palate and slipped down agreeably. Livened the discussion of my cases right up it did. Something needed to. It was either wine or a bomb.

"Just so happens I do know Florian. He applied for the Fire Service."

"Florian? Are you sure you've got the right man? The wee feardie runs off at the sight of a match."

His look said I was a halfwit. "With a name like that? Of course, it's the same bloke. Get a grip woman."

Fair point, but his rudeness stoked my temper up to white-hot flames. I damped it down and shuffled to the other end of the sofa. Larbert tried to grab me. I ducked his advances and said, "That's quite enough of that."

My stern tone penetrated my Lothario's passion and he sat back with a sigh.

"Florian?" I felt he needed a reminder just in case the passion had addled his brain a little.

"The man's a hose short of a fire engine."

I already knew that. "Any idea where he went after his deficiencies in the Fire Officer Department were legally noted and put down in writing?"

"How would I know. Do I look like the local branch of Jobseekers?"

With that, he was bundled out the door. "Don't come back unless you've any news on Florian." The door crashed, making me feel a lot better. The neighbours might not be quite so keen. They're all in bed by 9 pm round here, and you'd need a telescope to look back as far as that hour. Also, my door is about eight inches of solid oak. These houses were built to last way back when they had pots of money and no one worried about using up enough wood to strip an entire forest. On the building of one house.

The furry blanket ensconced in the middle of my bed refused to move despite cajoling, threats being muttered, and treats being waved. He snored blithely through the whole thing. I found a spare sheet, it being too hot for a duvet, curled up on the couch and pulled over a copy of the yellow pages. By the time I'd finished there were several numbers for dog training classes securely in my mobile phone. I was also drifting off.

That night's dreams were littered with multiple Florians wielding Fire Hoses and running into burning buildings. In a vague waking moment, I hoped that wasn't my subconscious telling me he'd shuffled off to the great fire station in the sky.

My next waking thought told me he was more likely burning on a beach in the Caribbean. The best route to a decent night's kip does not involve dreaming of Florian. From what I remembered of him from school he was the stuff of living nightmares. The lovely Kate's brains had to be stuffed with sausages to take up with him. Although I had already established that Kate wasn't exactly bright, so maybe their union made perfect sense. Either that or she liked the weight of his wallet. Especially when some of that weight made its way to her. In the form of several high-value notes.

31

About 5.30 a.m. my subconscious gave my conscious a kick in the teeth. I rocketed bolt upright in bed, wide awake, quickly realising the meaning of a cold sweat. I was tangled in a sheet and Eagal's head lay on my legs. When had he appeared? My general state of panic confused me until my brain caught up. If Florian was up to the top of his pointy ears in debt, that meant there were probably heavies out to abscond him as well. If they'd offed him, and I went poking my nose in, the logical trajectory meant they'd off me as well. This might, just might, be getting more serious than I could ever imagine. Maybe Mamah had a point re the suitability of my employment.

While Eagal munched, I danced. The soothing sounds of Mendelssohn's *A Midsummers Night's Dream* soon had me feeling much better about life. The pain in my knee was almost worth it. I winced. Almost. Finishing, I showered and dressed, deciding my ballet studio needed air conditioning. Top of the range it might be, but it was still hot as Hades. Who'd have thought Dundee could aspire to such temperatures, and for so long? if my memory served me well, Dundee's default weather zone involved rain. I'd become a right Southern Softie since moving to the metropolis.

A visit to the hospital called. I deposited the mutt with Quill, with strict instructions not to move. For any reason. I wasn't hopeful that either of them would be there on my return. Still, I had to at least speak like a boss. Pulp fiction detectives didn't take nonsense from anyone, especially employees. Not that they had many. Usually lone wolves.

My shoulders slumped at the next thought. They didn't have useless canine inheritances either. I cheered right up at the thought of a tough, Macintosh wearing, chain-smoking PI with a Chihuahua at his heels. The spring in my step added necessary speed to my journey.

I flashed an ID card that got me in through the doors of Kate's private room. Either the nurses were blind, or Quill's rendition of a police ID card was top notch. Yep, I'd resorted to subterfuge and my assistant's, quite excellent forging skills. How can I live with myself? Quite easily. It didn't actually say it was police. It quite clearly said, Private Investigator. Depending on your definition of clearly, of course. My eyesight is top notch.

Kate looked like a half-shut knife as they say around these parts. In her case maybe a quarter-shut knife. A blunt one. Despite this, she remained sharp on one point.

"I don't do drugs."

Taking a quick glance at her arms I agreed with every word. Not a track mark to be seen. Well, only one.

"So how come you were mainlining yesterday?"

This was so far out of my Royal Ballet comfort zone I'm surprised I knew the words.

"I didn't take drugs, mainlined or otherwise. The doorbell rang and when I opened it two masked men broke in."

Straight out of a cliché.

She must have taken in my incredulous look because she continued. "I'm telling the truth. One had a metal pipe in his hand." She closed her eyes for a few seconds.

I kept quiet. Got the best results when all's said and done.

"I think that's what it was. One whack and the next thing I know I've woken up here."

Shutting her eyes again, she lifted a feeble hand and rubbed the top of her head.

One tear slid down her cheek.

"They've told me I need to go through an addiction programme."

"From one use?"

Astonishment rendered me dumb.

"Is that possible."

"They say I probably won't be addicted, but best to be sure."

What an awful blow to be dealt by the hand of fate. All because she hooked up with a wastrel like Florian. I was almost frightened to mention his name. My case, and possible starvation, got the better of me. Yes, I know my mother feeds me, but why let the facts get in the way of a good story.

"Do you know where your boyfriend is?"

"Florian?"

How many boyfriends did she have? Maybe I was barking up the wrong set of gangsters here.

My voice tentative, I said, "Yes." Then added for good measure, "Unless you've any others."

She ignored the latter part of my questions. "I haven't heard from him in days."

More tears followed.

"Do you think they've got him?" she forced out through sobs.

I was sure they well and truly had him and busy praying hard he hadn't had *it*. Nevertheless, I said,

"Probably holed up in a hotel somewhere. He'll turn up bright and breezy when he runs out of money."

She looked particularly underwhelmed by my reassurances. Can't say I blamed her.

Time to change tack. Well, slightly.

"Any idea why he might have disappeared? If he's gone of his own accord."

"No."

This was like pulling whales' teeth only more difficult. I felt it an apt analogy considering Dundee's whaling past. Giving myself a mental high five, felt good. For a nanosecond.

Dragging myself out of my reverie I took in the strange look on Kate's face. It said, 'is this woman deranged.' She wasn't far wrong.

"How did he seem recently? Any change in mood. Did he seem shiftier?"

"Far from it. Happiest I've seen him in ages." Her eyelids drifted to the closed position.

"Kate!" My voice was sharper than it should have been.

"What?"

"His mood? Why was he so happy?"

"He said he had a fantastic business opportunity." Her eyes closed, but she dragged them open and focused. "Meant we could lead the life of Riley."

This time her eyes wouldn't open again.

I broke the news to the nursing staff that Kate was dozier than she should be. Or so I thought. My medical experience consisted of applying a bandage to the ankle of a seven-year-old dancer who tripped in a rehearsal for the Nutcracker. Badly applying I should add. First aid was not high on the list of priorities at the Royal

Ballet School. Applying cold compresses and arnica to sprains was about the extent of it. I pondered the wisdom of sending them an email informing them of their deficiencies.

A nurse hurtled off in Kate's direction. Another picked up the phone and spoke in a frantic voice. From this my PI brain surmised my news wasn't what they wanted to hear. Yet another nurse having corroborated Kate's story re the bump, I headed for my bike and the office.

Pretty much a straight run down the Perth Road, I was there before I knew it. Ready and raring to interrogate Quill. Or roast him over an open fire. Maybe both.

32

Much to my amazement, he was still there. Eagal on the other hand...

"What have you done with the pooch?" I glared at him. "I know I wanted rid of him, but that's my choice."

"Keep your tutu on. Your brother's taken him for a walk."

"Which one?" If it was Angus we'd never see either of them again. I'm not sure whether human or canine is the most reckless. The last time he took the dog for a ten-minute walk they'd ended up in Kirriemuir and I had to go rescue them.

"Lachlan. Said you'd ordered him to appear on the premises forthwith."

Did this bloke always have to use six words where one would do? Verbal diarrhoea is not an advanced skill in the PI world. I could feel some training coming on. If I ever got time to train myself never mind him. These cases were keeping my nose to the grindstone. Even if they weren't going anywhere, at least I was trying.

I dragged myself back to the room and Quill.

"If Lachie and the hellhound are gainfully employed, you and I can talk. Exactly where were you yesterday?"

"Pursuing a line of enquiry. I'd rather not say what at the moment."

I took three calming breaths then exploded anyway. "I take it you want to be doing a solo dance outside the employment office?"

"But—"

"Never mind 'but', what were you flaming well up to?"

"I really can't say."

As I drew in another deep breath he hurried on, "I don't want to place you in danger."

"What—?"

"I promise. The minute I can tell you I will."

He looked me straight in the eye. I stared straight back.

A few heartbeats later, wanting to believe him, I moved behind my desk and let the matter drop.

For now. Ballet dancers need good memories. My ability to faultlessly remember every step in a dance sequence would be put to good use in recalling this issue. His card, dance or otherwise, was marked.

I found myself wondering how my life had changed so radically. From culture and beauty to deranged dogs and batty employees, at the drunken twist of a stubborn steering wheel Not my drunken steering wheel, I hasten to add.

Ten minutes of silent contemplation later, Eagal charged through the door, almost taking it off its hinges. He leapt at me like I'd returned from a year's sojourn on the Desolation Islands. His joy at the reunion manifested itself in a vigorous washing of all my exposed skin. My tailored shorts and short sleeved blouse left a lot for him to explore.

"Eagal, no."

This resulted in renewed enthusiasm. The dumb animal spoke a different language to the rest of the canine population. I did the only thing I could, threw a treat at the skirting board. A thump, the wall shook and Eagal settled down with his treat.

I took in my brother's shaking body and could almost see him swallowing laughter.

"Big bobby like you might have waded into help, never mind stand there laughing."

"No chance. I was having way too much fun. That dog should be designated a public health and safety hazard."

"Have at it. Then you can arrest him."

"If you think I'm taking that brute up the nick, you're barking up the wrong closie. My mates would never forgive me."

"Lachie Claymore, I'll be telling mamah you're a useless waste of police time."

Quill interrupted our sparring and witty repartee with a couple of short coughs. We both turned and glared at him.

"Sparkling though your conversation is, I'm fascinated by the reason your brother is here."

Lachie smiled at Quill.

I scowled at Lachie. "He's right. Stop wasting my time."

He raised one economical eyebrow. "You asked me here."

"Stop gnashing your gums. I need a favour."

Lachie sat down, put one jean-clad leg over the other, one nonchalant arm on the back of the chair and rolled his eyes.

Ignoring him I ploughed on. "What do you know about Florian?"

Yet again I was observing the 'are you half-baked?' look. "The idiot we went to school with?"

"The very one and the same. How many Florian's can there be in Dundee, you stupid sod?"

"What do you want with that useless lump of lard?

147

He's a tattie scone short of a Scottish Breakfast."

"Seems our Florian's quite the hunk now. He's also up to his hunky ears in debt." I paused for a heartbeat. Dramatic effect can work wonders in the PI world. "And missing."

33

I could almost hear the cogs in Lachie's brain grinding. Then he burst out laughing. "Who the heck cares? The man's a scourge on humanity."

"Lachlan Claymore, I'm shocked. His sister cares."

"How come you're so pally with her all of a sudden? Didn't she pull your pigtails or something?" He wiped tears from his eyes.

I wondered if he was on drugs. "Ha, flaming ha. Pay attention. She wants him found. Our views on their entire extended family withstanding, I need him to be alive, well and annoying everyone again."

"How much is she paying you?"

Blast, he knew me too well. "Never you mind. Are you going to help, or what?"

"Do your own work, you lazy besom."

"What do you think I'm doing?" I gazed at him with a steely calm. Well, that's what I told myself anyway. I probably looked more like someone who'd escaped from Carstairs.

"Can you do a check on him and tell me if he's got form?"

The annoying git threw his head back and almost choked on his laughter. "Have you been watching cop shows again?" He sobered up enough to say, "He's done nothing. No way I'm looking him up."

I wished he had choked on his laughter. *No way he was getting away with this.* "Remember, his girlfriend's up the hospital. Smacked over the head and pumped full of drugs." I resorted to half-truths. "Florian could be implicated."

"How come I'm only hearing about this now?"

"You heard about it yesterday. You were in her flat."

I watched the light dawn on Lachie's face, closely followed by storm clouds descending. Poetic. In a horror-struck kind of way.

My pen holder rattled with the force of his next words. "And you didn't tell me this before?"

"Didn't think it was important." Subterfuge and lying seemed to be coming rather easily. I preferred to call it cunning and wile. Lachie might call it a criminal offence, but we weren't splitting words here.

"Cass Claymore, I've a mind to arrest you for obstructing or hindering a police officer."

"You might want to reread the law books. Refusing to give information isn't obstruction."

That was when he lost it big time. His actual words? Not suitable for repetition before a general audience. They lasted a long time and ended with, "...not a damn thing is what I'm going to do."

I headed in the direction of the kitchen and poured him a nice cup of Java.

Grasping the bone china mug in his hands he inhaled and sipped it. Slowly.

I gave the balm a few minutes to work its magic and then said, "I really need your help on this, Lachie. Just a quick peep."

There was that wheedle peeping out again. I was willing to let it show its face if it helped me receive assistance from the boys in blue.

"I'll think about it." In Lachie speak this meant, consider it done.

My shoulders slumped in relief. I put up a hand to my aching neck and massaged it. This job had unforeseen consequences. Tender muscles being one of them. Used to aching legs and arms, come on I'm a ballet dancer, this took it to a whole new level.

I had the sudden urge to perform an arabesque, followed by a devéloppé and a grande rond du jambe. That would loosen me up. It would also soothe my frazzled nerves.

Lachie's next words turned my thoughts to GBH rather than exercise. Yes, I know there's no such thing as GBH in Scotland, but who's arguing.

"If that's all the little princess needs, I'm off to do some real work." He unfolded himself from the chair and headed for the door. Another languid wave and he disappeared. I threw a pencil sharpener after him. Somehow it wasn't quite satisfying enough. It rattled on the floor and the pooch leapt after it. Not quite making it I watched the pencil sharpener disappear down his gullet.

Good grief. With visions of ripped intestines dancing in my head, I phoned Alexander for advice.

Rather than rushing over to help and assist he told me off for being so careless. Then he told me to keep a close eye on the pooch. And all dog pooh for the next two or three days.

"Is that it?"

"Cass, I've been treating that blasted animal since it was suckling at its mother's teats. It's eaten more rubbish than you'll ever know about. Give me a ring if you're worried."

"Fine." I still wasn't convinced.

"Must fly. I've a five-year-old worried about a pet mouse."

"Your brother seems like a useful chap to know. Extremely helpful."

"Which brother?"

Quill frowned in puzzlement. "The one who was just here."

"If you know what buttons to press."

"You seem particularly adept at this, my dear."

"Years of practice. You'll never reach that level of skill."

"I fear I won't."

I wasn't so sure.

34

"Unhelpful…"

The phone rang before I could finish my profound statement. It was my dad.

"Mrs McLellan's looking for you?"

McLellan was my English teacher back in secondary school. I still came out in a sweat at the very thought of a dangled participle never mind a rogue comma. The woman would have Vlad the Impaler sitting at his desk with his arms crossed. What on earth did she want with me?

I asked my father that very question.

"How would I know. Phone the old bat."

He rattled off a number, then left me listening to the strident tone of a discontinued conversation. Charming.

I'd forgotten he'd had the same English teacher. By my reckoning, she must be about 180 years old. Actually, that was her age when she taught me. So maybe a conservative estimate of her current age.

"You've turned a rather peculiar shade of pale, Cassandra."

Too weak to respond I picked up the phone and dialled the number.

It was answered faster than I would have liked.

"Miss Claymore. Thank you for ringing."

I'd managed to forget McLellan's flair for utilising the more eccentric aspects of Miss Jean Brodie. Her cultured Scottish brogue brought the memories rushing back. Adrenaline pumped through my veins as I recalled our last encounter. This had involved illicit ballet moves, a pot of ink and McLellan's Sunday dress. I shivered.

"You wanted to speak to me?"

"Of course I did, you stupid girl. It would appear your brain is still addled."

The metallic taste of blood reminded me to release my teeth from their death grip on my tongue. I stared at Quill, who had an enquiring look in his eye. Too traumatized to even chuck a dirty look in his direction, I didn't respond.

She continued. "It would appear dear Dave has got himself embroiled in something."

I shook my head. Vigorously. It cleared the fog and allowed a cogent response. "Dave?"

"Stallins. Are you a halfwit?"

My schooldays were long gone. As were Dave's. This unexplained concern for his welfare seemed out of character for Attila the Nun as we used to call her. Not that she was, but the nearest thing you'd get without entering a convent.

My silence must have indicated my puzzlement.

"He's my godson."

TMI. If I hadn't been sitting Reeling would have occurred. Yes, with a capital R.

I made a passable imitation of a goldfish. If she could see it my knuckles would be red raw from the swift application of a well-aimed ruler. Flying dry board dusters also featured in her torture repertoire if I remembered correctly.

"Hello. Are you still there?"

The familiar gravelly voice yanked me back from the brink.

"I'm not sure what I can do to help."

"You'll have a word with him of course. Sort it out."

A familiar tone filled my ears. Jeez, could no one say ta-ta around here?

Shutting my eyes, I leaned back in my chair. When I opened them, Quill stood next to me with a glass of water.

"Good grief. That's the last thing a woman needs."

His brows furrowed. "Water? I could go and fetch a restorative bottle of wine if you would rather."

"No, eejit. Mrs McLellan."

I took the glass, drank deeply, and filled him in. By the time I'd finished, tears poured down his face.

"The best laugh I've had in ages. So, what are you going to do about dear Dave?"

"Nothing. That's what we're going to do. Nothing."

Quill took two steps back. "I take it ballet dancers need powerful lungs."

"I've had enough of your lip. Shove off."

I stomped off in the direction of the kitchen, tempted to put a slug of gin in my coffee. Shame I didn't have any about my person. I wondered if there was any turps left from the office makeover and dreamt of the Shiraz waiting for me to put it out of its misery in my kitchen.

I considered sending Quill out to buy a bottle of something. There was an Off Licence next door, and for a seedy operation it carried some nice wines. I could start the Shiraz now and instruct my assistant in the finer points of drinking wine. If he worked for me it's a skill he would require.

Then common sense took over. If a miracle occurred, and a new client turned up, it wasn't a good look if everyone in the agency was roaring drunk. Us Scots have a reputation for being a nation of drunkards. I didn't want to perpetuate the myth. Or ruin my uncle's inheritance.

35

Despite my vehemence, I had a strong suspicion Dave Stallins was of great import. Smack bang in the midst of everything. Which meant I didn't have the option of doing nothing. I slammed a couple of cupboard doors. This had the effect of snapping a hinge and making my temper worse. I decided chamomile tea might soothe my frazzled nerves.

How one went about finding someone like Dave was another investigation altogether. He and I didn't march to the same drumbeat. Which got me thinking about exactly why he was so intimate with the details of my life. Like I had a new career. It wasn't exactly emblazoned across the front of the *Evening Telegraph*, Dundee or any other edition. My blood froze at the thought Mr Weasel might just be stalking me.

It was time to pull on the Old Girls network to see if anyone had a scoobie. Mind you, most women ran a mile at the very thought of Desperate Dave. Hence his nickname.

I started with the lovely Mimosa.
"Get on with your effing job without persecuting me." Slammed phone. Well, as slammed as a mobile got.
Charming! I rather felt that persecuting her was one of the perks of the job.
I dialled her number again.
"For heaven's sake. What do you want?"
"Is Florian friends with Dave Stallins?"

"Who the eff is he?"

I had a feeling darling Mimosa's turn of phrase might
be one of the major reasons for her being rejected for
the Royal Ballet. She swore like a tinker even when she
was at primary school. That, and the fact her dancing
didn't quite meet the standard. I'm being polite here.
Her attitude derrière was more attitude debacle, her
relevé in fifth could barely be considered a fourth and,
more to the point, her pointes were duller than one of
Attila the Nun's English lessons.

"Desperate Dave from primary school."

"How the flaming heck would I know. I haven't seen
the weasel since we left school, thank God. You need a
life, Claymore."

"He could be tied up in your Brother's disappearance.
Haven't got any contact details for him by any
chance?"

My voice had taken on a soupcon of pleading. I hated
it. Even Eagal sensed my desperation. He sat up, gave
my hand a reassuring lick and put a paw on my knee.
Bless. I pulled a treat from my pocket and gave him it.
He flopped down again to save energy for chewing it.
Comforting someone is hard work. Obviously.

I turned my attention back to the phone call.

"You have got to be joking. I wouldn't touch him if
he was the only man alive."

She raised a valid point. The only one on which she
and I agreed.

I scored through the first name on my list.

My primary school was huge. Contact numbers for
most of them eluded me, meaning the numbers
dwindled. Ninety-four minutes into my search I hit
mother lode.

"Yep. Saw him last week."

A couple of minutes of 'how are you's?' and 'what are you up to's?', and I had a mobile number for the weasel himself. Score.

It didn't turn out to be such a score when I rang him. He didn't answer. Surely, as a result of his stalking, he'd know it was me and rush to my aid. Git. Time to bring in the big guns.

I'd elicited, from my school chum, that our Dave still lived with his decrepit mum. In a flat at the far end of Whitfield. Too far to walk. Leaving Quill with a pile of searches and the shaggy rug, I was soon feeling the breeze on my face as the bike bore me towards the other end of town. What a glorious feeling and a glorious day to be alive. Being an investigator wasn't that bad after all.

Graffiti and peeling paint told my keen investigator mind the flats were as decrepit as Dave's mum. Or so I thought. The opened door had my jaw in a downward trajectory and almost smacking off the floor. Dave's mum was a new woman. So much so, I wondered if it was his mother at all.

"Cass Claymore, as I live and breathe. Come in, hen."

Yep, definitely the Glaswegian Mrs Stallins. I can't believe she remembered me. Maybe she was stalking me as well.

"I've been followin' you in the papers. Dundee's poster girl. Yer ma must be proud."

My mouth refused to utter a word in response.

She lifted her hand and patted her bouffant hair. "I'm a changed wuman. Wee Davie's paid for me tae have plastic surgery." Her taut face twitched into what could be considered a smile. "I can see yer surprised."

Plastic surgery didn't come cheap. Not even in Dundee. Where was the weasel getting enough dosh to tart up his dear old ma?

Come to think of it, why would he want to chuck fistfuls of cash at his ma? He never struck me as the filial type. More the grab everything you can type.

Ushered into the living room, I waited while the plastic poodle made tea. I could feel a sofa spring poking into my jacksie. The rest of the furniture was also dilapidated. Desperate Dave's largesse didn't stretch to providing furniture. I pulled out my phone and jotted down a reminder to look into the matter. Of his sudden affluence and the plastic surgery. Not the furniture.

Dave's ma was happy to natter about her wee laddie.

"He's a good lad. Spent a' this money on me. Is that no' nice o' him?"

I thought it was more than nice. Didn't sound like the Dave I knew from school. Unless he'd found religion, there was more to this than meets the eye.

"What's Dave doing these days?"

"He's got a good job. Up in Aberdeen. Earning more each month than his dad made in a whole a year."

If memory served me, Dave's dad was on the dole and his mother worked three jobs to feed them all. The hardest work he did was lifting a pint down a pub as seedy as the Duck and Dagger.

"Amazing. Good for him. I'd like to speak to him."

I took a sip of my tea, which more resembled water. I got the impression she just waved the tea bag at lukewarm water.

"He gave me a good referral and I got a great job from it. I'd like to buy him a drink to say thanks."

"He'd love that. Let me get you the number." She

jumped up and bustled off.

I shifted on the sofa and found an even more intimate spring. Lifting one cheek gave a small measure of comfort.

By the time she returned, both cheeks had gone to sleep. I'd also managed to revive a pot plant with the remainder of my tea and entertained myself by stopping a somewhat frisky black cat from having its wicked ways with my leathers.

"Where did that thing come from?"

"The bedroom I think. Strolled through the door like the Goddess Bastet."

I tickled it behind the ears.

"She's gorgeous."

"That's no' my cat. Who's bas... whatsit?"

"Egyptian feline Goddess."

A glaikit look appeared in her eyes. Egyptian history not her strong point then. If her IQ was anything like her son's, she wouldn't have many strong points.

We both stared at the offending animal. It sat primly, gazing back with a 'what you gonna do about it' look on its face.

Kind to animals as well as her wee laddie, she gently shoved it to one side with the toe of her slipper. The cat jumped up on a chair, turned around three times, curled up and settled down for a kip.

She handed over a sheet of paper. "I've given you his address. Never been, but I think it's some swanky place. Up in Aberdeen."

If Dave was up to his unmentionables in dodgy goings on, then his mother being so free with his whereabouts would have him in difficulty quicker than you could say crook. Especially since mummy dearest had never been to visit. In Scotland that was telling.

I said goodbye and left Mrs Stallins to her primping and preening. I hopped on the bike and the engine roared into life. A wee visit to Aberdeen beckoned.

36

Phoning Quill, I learned he was gainfully occupied. Doing what, I didn't dare ask. Blithely leaving him and the hellhound to their own devices I belted up the A90 towards Aberdeen. It was a grand life right enough.

I whistled when I got to Desperate Dave's house. He certainly had gone upmarket. His apartment building had a concierge, gym and swimming pool. There wouldn't be much change out of half a million squids. If that.

Let me put my astonishment into context. When we are at school, Dave set himself the lowest standards and never managed to achieve them. How had he gone from that to a millionaire's bachelor pad in the swankiest area of Aberdeen?

A quick flash of my fake warrant card and the concierge ushered me towards the lift. He employed a security card and I was soon rocketing towards the penthouse apartment. This lift made absolutely no noise. Eerie. Gave the impression of teleporting.

Stepping onto a cream carpet with pile so thick they'd have to send out a search party to find you again, I knocked on the door.

I waited then hammered loudly, secretly wondering if my journey had been wasted.

No way I was leaving. I sank to the ground, leaned against the pristine wall, and settled in for the wait.

I didn't have to wait long. The door opened, and Dave stood there wearing nothing but a pair of red silk boxers. They left nothing to the imagination. He scratched his head and peered at me.

"Well, well. Cass Claymore."

Some more scratching this time in places I don't want to discuss. Let's leave it at the fact Dave had not changed.

"How did you find me?"

"You might want to tell your mother not to be so free with your personal data."

I took one step forward and put my hand on the door.

"She's a wee bit too chatty if you get my gist."

I pushed the door gently. It stood firm. I shoved harder.

"Are you not going to invite a girl in? I wasn't expecting red carpet treatment, but at least a cup of coffee."

"Do you think I'm running a café here or something?"

"Davey, Davey. I've come all the way from Bonnie Dundee to see you. The least you can do is pony up a drink. Your ma would be ashamed of you."

A woman appeared at his back. Scantily dressed, it was obvious I'd interrupted something important.

"Now I understand your reluctance. I'd still like a chat. I'm sure Blondie here will keep the bed warm for you."

"Lareen, time to skedaddle. Fetch your stuff. Your money will be ready."

The girl's eyes filled with tears.

His tone softened somewhat. "I'll give you a ring later. We'll go clubbing."

Tears having magically disappeared, Lareen followed them with the vanishing act.

I shoved the door hard pulling it out of Dave's hand and

smashing it against the wall. Without a by your leave, I strolled inside.

I love this private detecting lark. It gives me carte blanche to do and say exactly what I want. The pulp fiction PIs would be proud. My mother on the other hand…

I'd had enough of this and was as dry as a prohibition bar. I charged into the kitchen and rustled around in cupboards. There was less in there than mine. How could that even possible?

Having got rid of the prossie, or girlfriend if he insisted, Dave did some charging of his own. The tiny kitchen suddenly became crowded. This wasn't a flat intended for cooking or anything else a kitchen might be used for. With Davey involved, I didn't like to speculate.

I picked up the kettle and shook it. Yep, enough for one cup of coffee. I slammed it back on the stand and switched it on.

"What the hell are you doing?"

"Making myself a drink. You're not exactly rolling out the red carpet."

"Shove off."

"For someone so keen to see me gainfully employed, you're doing a grand job of trying to shove me out the door."

I returned to my coffee making duties. In the spirit of goodwill, I made one for my host as well. Us Claymores are a kind lot.

"So, Davey boy. What's all this about the new job?"

"What's it to do you with you, Ging."

"Very grown-up. It's got lots to do with me, seeing as you seem to be in the middle of my latest case."

"Latest case! It's your only case."

"How come you know so much about me and my business?"

I shook a finger at him.

"Anyways you're out of date. I've landed another one."

"Wouldn't you like to know?" His weasel eyes narrowed. "Cut to the chase, Ging, I'm in a hurry."

"Tell me all about your flash new job then."

'Mind your own."

"If your business is legit why're you so keen to keep schtum? What you got to hide?"

He shook his head. "If I answer will you buzz off?"

"Depends on your answer. I'm trained to keep pushing."

"You're not trained at all." I could see the wheel turning but wasn't sure the hamster was in residence. Finally, he said, "I'm working for Lord Lamont. I'm his right-hand man."

The term Bantam Cock leapt to mind once more. There seemed to be a lot of chicken impressions going on amongst the males in this case.

"The gig pays well then?" A statement more than a question.

His surroundings gave me my answer. I wasn't sure what other questions to ask to be honest. I was floundering like a newbie in the corps de ballet.

"Top dollar."

"What's with all the dosh spent on your mother's upgrade?"

I looked him straight in the eye.

"It's weird isn't it, a son paying for his ma's plastic surgery. Bit creepy if you ask me."

His eyes darkened to Satan black. "No one asked you anything. She's always wanted it. What's weird about that?"

"I've always wanted a Porche. Do you fancy buying me one?"

He did the mature thing and stared in the other direction. Then slammed his mug on the table.

"You should mind that temper, Davey Boy."

This did not go down well. I could see his fists curling. Time to move the conversation along. He was always a bit free with his fists.

"So how do I get a job with eye-watering amounts of pay funded by the Laird?"

"You've got one. Although I'm beginning to regret throwing your name in the ring."

"How many other names were in the ring?"

"You were chosen from a cast of thousands."

"None then?"

"That's about right."

I slammed my coffee cup down on the rosewood table in a good imitation of Dave. Someone had the good sense to cover it in Perspex. When did the slovenly Davey become so fancy in his furniture choices? And his clothing. Sporting tailored shorts, well-pressed shirt and expensive brogues, he'd scrubbed up well.

Leaning back in my chair I said, "Where do you think the teddy is?"

I caught a hint of something dark in his eyes before it disappeared and was replaced by a false smile. It reminded me of a dodgy car salesman.

"It's an auld teddy. The rugrat could have lost it anywhere."

"So, why have the aristocracy got me chasing my tail looking for it?"

The weasel look reappeared.

"Roderic got fed up with the wife's nagging and the

brat's screaming."

Roderic sounded like a right bundle of laughs. It was about time I had a word with him.

One wee problem. I had no clue where the exalted Lord might be, or how to find him. Everyone was so keen to keep me away from Roderic I couldn't even speak to him in his own house. You'd think he'd be keen to hand over any information so his son and her would once more have peace. Nope, our Roderic was too busy doing his own thing.

"Top of your head, possible places to find the missing antique?"

A staring match ensued. I lost.

"I'm growing bored here. Come on, spit it out. You owe me one. In fact, you owe me several for all the times I stuck up for you in school."

A hint of wheedling crept into my tone. I tamed my inner wheedle and said, in a stern voice. "Surely you wouldn't hang me out to dry?"

I narrowed my eyes for good effect.

The wheedling or the sternness did the trick. Either that or he was fed up listening to me. He rattled off a few likely places.

I'd never heard of any of them. It looked like I'd be paying homage to the god, Google. I was becoming rather nifty on the old search engine and thought I might start selling classes in it.

"You'll be going now?"

That was my cue, and this time he insisted on compliance.

I could tell he was insistent by the force of his grip on my arm. Employing a few tricks I'd learnt (you don't live in London without them) I twisted and ducked. I was soon free and turning the tables. Nicely. If I'd wanted to play badly I could do it in a heartbeat. Everyone underestimates the strength of a ballet dancer.

37

I can be really stubborn when I want to be.

Going? You have to be joking. On a roll, I decided to go for broke.

"Not so fast Mr Fancy Pants. What's your relationship with Florian McIntosh?"

A look flickered over his eyes and darted off again. I could swear it was fear.

"What are you implying?"

"Mind that blood pressure of yours. I'm asking if you're still in touch with him, not if the pair of you are having an affair."

His shoulders relaxed. Interesting. Looked like I'd hit on something the pair didn't want waved about in public. Score 1 to the PI

"Not that it's any of your business, but we kept in touch."

"When did you last see him?"

"A couple of months ago. We went for a pint." His voice took on a falsetto squeak.

He was lying like a cheap Chinese watch. Yes, I'd read a book on body language whilst in the desert phase of my new role. Changes in the voice indicated the speaker was lying. Apparently.

"You may want to rethink that, Davey." I put one nonchalant knee over another and leaned back on the couch. "Your old ma wouldn't be happy to know you're telling porky pies."

He jumped up, stormed over to an antique cabinet, and poured himself a scotch from a crystal decanter. A large one. One quick swallow and it was gone.

Whirling around he said, "Get out of here. Now. I've had enough."

And *I'd* had enough of this back and forth chat. "Now listen here, Willy Weasel. I don't care what you do in your spare time, but Florian is M.I.A. So, if you want to see him again, you'd better start talking."

The squeak was back. "What? Why? How? What's it to you?"

"Mimosa is paying me good hard cash to find her missing brother. You don't want to get on the wrong side of the piranha now, do you?"

This had the intended effect. My nemesis terrified the whole school back in the day. Also, she'd be livid that her brother was batting for both sides. Apparently. Did I tell you Mimosa is a right snob? She's the only person in Dundee who would give a flying fig about the matter.

This effectively loosened his tongue. He'd seen Florian three days before. Interesting. This shortened the timeline of his disappearance by several days. What was our Florian hiding, apart from his alleged sexuality? Were the girlfriends cover-ups on both their parts? Why were they covering anything up?

Too many questions buzzing around my head. And I was willing to stake my business on the fact that Desperate Dave wouldn't answer any of them.

I gave it a go anyway. PI's don't get results by using an adagio – slow and careful. Allegro – fast and furious – was more the order of the day.

Channelling my inner brash I said, "If you want to see Florian again you'd better start answering questions."

I leaned forward and looked him straight in the eye. Then I paused for dramatic effect.

"What is Florian up to?"

There it was. The look that brought rabbits and headlights to mind. Davey, up to his armpits in deadly doings, was a right feardy on the strength of it.

The next words out of his mouth changed my mind pretty fast.

The rabbit changed to a lion.

"Where the f…"

He drew a deep breath.

"Ma taught me not to swear in front of a lady. Not that I think you're one."

He leaned forward as well, so we were practically eyeballing each other over the coffee table.

"This is my home and you're trespassing. One more word out of your mouth and Florian won't be the only one missing."

This was turning serious. My immediate instinct - flee. But I needed to man, or woman, up.

Shoving my hands between my knees to stop them trembling I said, "Are you threatening me?"

"Friendly advice. Take that sticky beak of yours and shove it somewhere else. Preferably up your own asshole."

He stood. "It's time for you to leave."

Before I could say investigate I was yanked from the chair and bundled towards the door.

He finished by saying, "Remember, don't bother Roderic.

"Of course not. Wouldn't dream of it."

As the lift whisked me downwards I knew with all my being, I fully intended bothering Roderic. With bells on. He was next on my list to visit today.

I left wondering why everyone was so keen to keep the exalted Lord Lamont out of the picture. Surely he couldn't be that much of an ogre that the whole world wanted me to stay away from him. My brilliant detective mind turned over all the possibilities as to what dear Roderic might actually be up to. Every fibre of my being shouted at me that the exalted Lord was right up to his royal neck in dodgy dealings.

The Pulp fiction detectives whispered in my ear that my next conversation should be with the Laird. I fully intended taking their advice. Who am I to argue with the experts.

38

The Lord's estate was locked up tighter than an otter's pocket. I rattled the front gate so hard the Lamont family crest slipped slightly. Whoops. Mental note add vandalism to my CV. No give from the lock.

Wondering if the picks I was about to receive would work on a two-hundred-year-old lock, I rang the buzzer on the gatepost. Several times. With increasing vigour and length. I'm surprised I didn't waken the royal ancestors, all tucked up nice and cosy in the castle cemetery. Yep, a private cemetery. And a chapel. I'd looked the place up online.

Standing back, I took in my surroundings. Thick walls about three times my height, solid stone with gates firmly attached. No wriggle room to slip through. Considering they protected an ancient castle, the walls looked well maintained. This part of them anyway.

Ringing the bell again, I considered how no one could be home in a castle. There must be a brace or more servants of some ilk loitering in the hallways. Saying that, if they'd left Billy the Butler at home either deafness or infirmity would slow down the door opening.

A beautiful day turning into a warm evening, the scent of wildflowers hovered in the air, soporific in a non-poppy sort of way. The chirrup of birds added to the impression of an Alexander Nasmyth landscape. They give you a thorough grounding in all the arts at The Royal Ballet School, so I'm well versed in these things.

That, and the fact one of my Claymore ancestors was best pals with the man himself. We've one hanging up at home. I'm surprised one of the Claymore minors haven't chucked a missile at it, but it remains remarkably preserved.

A sound, gentle but discordant, tickled my eardrums. It took my brain a few seconds to catch up before my head jerked in its general direction. Nothing. Shading my eyes with my hand, I stared harder. There. I could see, just about, a security camera. Taking a couple of steps to the right, I watched as it followed me. Time to leave methinks. But there was no way I could leave this to chance. In someone else's immortal words, I'd be back.

39

The trip back allowed valuable thinking time. I stayed on the right side of the law in terms of speed and light jumping. There were only so many times I could go nose to nose with Bacon and come out winning. Even Lachie's protection only stretched so far.

I returned to Armageddon. My office looked like the Highland Light Infantry had charged through on their way to a skirmish. Upturned chairs and a desk standing at a rakish angle were not how I'd envisaged my return.

Quill was nowhere to be seen. The only occupant, a rather dazed Lady Lucy sitting on the one chair remaining in its rightful position. Her infant had also vanished if the empty buggy was anything to go by. Today she wore a tasteful peach suit by Balenciaga with another stunning Rosie Olivia original atop her curls. The price of her outfit alone would keep Eagal in dog food for a year.

"Lady Lamont—"

The words were whipped from my brain and my mouth as a lanky seven-year-old rushed into the room arms akimbo and making engine noises. Loudly. He was followed by a screaming toddler and a harried Quill who resembled The Wreck of the Hesperus. Eagal followed the toddler, gently keeping an eye on him.

I assumed the blonde moppet, wearing nothing but his birthday suit, was Theo. He stopped short, took one look at me, grinned, parked his chubby toddler bottom on the parquet flooring, and peed. His being a boy, it did not go well. The resulting spray involved a large area of floor, the wall, and his face.

I instantly understood the reason for the uproar.

"Hezzie, sit down this instance."

"Don' wanna." He resumed his aeroplane impression.

Yanking his collar, I forced his backside into contact with the leather of my desk chair.

"That's assault."

"Listen here, street lawyer, one more move and I'll tie you to the chair."

He opened his mouth.

"Then I'll tell your father why I did it."

That effectively shut him up. Percy's husband, a stalwart of the community, is the only one who can keep Hezekiah in check. The fact he works in Perth Prison helps. Although I'd take my chances with a tattooed, steroid-fuelled inmate over Hezzie any day.

I would be having strong words with my sister about her using my office as a crèche.

"Why aren't you at school?" I hauled a chair upright and slammed it down.

"No school on a Saturday, silly." He swivelled his chair round and round. "Schools borin'."

I grabbed the seat, halting its momentum. "You'll make yourself sick."

His look told me I was a batty old spoilsport. I'd seen that sullen look before and it did not bode well.

"Where's the rest of your family?" My voice brooked no nonsense.

"Dunno."

Surly little beggar. He was far too young for the teenage approach.

Quill, having straightened himself up to his usual

dapper self, assisted me with putting the furniture back to rights. Lady Lucy cleaned up both the floor and her progeny before dressing him in a nappy. Initially resistant, he cried himself to sleep in her lap. She looked as exhausted as the bratling.

I made a mental note to engage the services of Aunty Morag and a bottle of Clorox. An office that smelled like the public toilet didn't endear one to one's clients.

I poured coffee for us all and settled the flea bag down with treats. The mini thug was threatened with GBH if he moved a muscle. He busied himself chewing a huge packet of toffees I had loafing in the drawer. He could exercise all his excessive energy moving his jaws. Plus, the added bonus, it would shut him up.

Raising an enquiring eyebrow, I stared at Quill.

His IQ actually being somewhere north of Mensa, he caught on quickly. Why he'd turned to a life of crime was a total mystery to me.

"His mother asked if I could undertake caretaker duties for the boy. How could I refuse such a delightful lady?"

How could anyone use so many words to say Percy dumped my nephew here?

"Have you heard of the word, no?"

Quill matched my eyebrow and raised me two.

His argument was a good one. My sister didn't know the meaning of the word no and carried on regardless.

I still wasn't having it. Where did he get off deciding that we would provide a playground for every waif and stray this side of the Tay Bridge? How was I meant to run a business with the place cluttered up with kids who thought they were a one-man terrorist group?

My look told him we'd be discussing the matter in depth the minute my client took her designer-clad and possibly surgically enhanced bottom through my office door. His decision-making skills needed some measure of polishing.

Hezzie recommenced his birling in the seat. He was making me dizzy.

"One more twirl and I'll feed you to the dog. My tone was stern, the only version which worked with the wee monster. Thank the good Lord that at least the dog appeared fast asleep. Not even the rogue twitch of a floppy ear indicated he was listening in.

"Ahem!"

My client's equilibrium had not only returned but with renewed attitude.

"Sorry, what can I do for you?"

She shifted the sleeping baby and stared at me. It would appear we were playing the waiting game again. What is it with these people that they can't just spit out the answer without dramatic pauses and thinking time. As she'd come to me it wasn't the most difficult question in the world to answer. I wasn't exactly asking her to explain the origin of black holes.

My stare jolted her into action. She ran her tongue round her pearlescent peach lipsticked lips and opened her mouth displaying a set of gnashers the glitterati would pay good money for.

Quill and I leaned forward in anticipation. This had better be good or I swear, cheque or no cheque, I'd kick her to the middle of next week and back, dumping her at a different agency en route.

"It would appear that my husband has also gone missing."

40

What did one say to that? Especially something that didn't involve the words sign a bigger cheque.

I really needed to work on that enigmatic thing, as Lady Lucy immediately rummaged in her bag. A chequebook and fountain pen appeared, and the cheque was duly filled in and signed.

Almost snatching it from her hand, I took in the amount and pocketed it in about one-hundredth of a second. A rush to the bank job if I ever saw one. The manager would throw me a party. Or report me for money laundering.

The laird would soon be barasic if she carried on chucking cash at me.

I tossed Hezzie out of my chair and instructed him to sit beside Eagal and not move. All the birling must have worn him out because he curled up beside the dog and was snoring in minutes. Blimey, that was a first.

Pulling a yellow legal pad over, I said, "Details." Short, to the point and business-like took over from polite. I hoped my assistant was taking notes on how I handled this and the brevity of my speech.

Lucinda didn't think much of my brevity. She conveyed this to me by one superior curl of a sophisticated lip.

Politeness over brevity then. Okay. No one can accuse me of not being quick on the uptake.

"When did you last see your husband?"

No sooner were the words out of my mouth than I had a sudden urge to giggle. I had visions of the Yeames painting, 'When did you Last see your Father'? Although this wasn't quite the civil war. Yet.

I reined in my trembling lips and looked halfway solemn. Laughing at vanishing husbands wasn't the way to earn repeat custom or heartfelt recommendations.

"Two days ago." Her words were terse.

This brevity thing was going too far. In order for me to find all her missing accoutrements, she needed to spill, and spill fast. I couldn't help but feel her ability to misplace anything near and dear to her was unfortunate. I worried about the safety of little Theo. If she was batting for three, then the logical conclusion meant he was the next one to perform a little disappearing act. From teddies to a Lord of the Realm seemed a stretch even for this batty case.

The story went as follows.

It had all gone down three nights ago. Theo, screaming for his cherished Teddy refused to go to bed. A full-blown toddler tantrum followed, including toy chucking and extreme banging. Anyone who's ever cared for a toddler will know where I'm coming from.

Roderic had a few chums over, and the tiny heir to the throne was disturbing them. Perish the thought his darling offspring should interfere with all the bonhomie and backslapping, or whatever the toffs got up to in their spare time. He stormed out of his office and shouted at the moppet at which point Lady Lucy stepped in. This hadn't gone down well with the Lord of the Manor, and he and his chums, tipsy to a man, started throwing their weight around. Clint, still employed despite Lucy's best efforts, whipped them up further.

Fenella, despite ten-foot-thick walls, somehow heard the rumpus and trotted downstairs to join in the general shouting match. It was at this point all hell let loose. Yes, more hell than they already had within those hallowed halls.

Theo, tired and fed up with being ignored, toddled up to one of his dad's chums grabbed his leg, and then bit him, hard enough to draw blood. This did not go down well and resulted in the man slapping Theo round the head. At this point, Fenella showed her true colours and used a loafing riding crop to whack him hard across the face. Turns out the teen was keener on the sproglet than she let on.

Thus ensued another chase around the dining room involving Fenella, her father, and one enraged chum whilst the other men cheered and took bets on who would win. Fenella being young, fit and sober, and the others drunk as a fox in an apple barrel, she was able to keep well out of their way, until she tripped over the upturned end of a Kashmir Pure Silk Rug. Lady Lucy was clear on the exact make. Anyway, I digress. Fenella ended up with a broken arm. Whether from her father, the trip or the chum wasn't quite clear. My bet went on a mixture of all three.

Mama Bear was fonder of her stepdaughter than she wanted to admit because she stepped into the fray. This resulted in another black eye if the makeup was anything to go by. She wasn't as forthcoming on this point.

The nanny who'd started the entire process stood back and wailed. Theo wailed louder, resulting in the nanny being sacked. She fled to her room leaving Lady Lucy to look after a toddler and an injured teen, which didn't go down well with her employer.

At this point, Roderic dragged his mates out the impressive front door and hadn't been seen since.

41

I was exhausted just listening to this tale of woe. My take on the matter - Roderic and his mates were still drinking themselves senseless in a high-end hotel somewhere. My personal view, she was better off without him.

Throughout I had been watching Quill. His quivering lips indicated laughter was about to erupt, faster and harder than any volcano. My piercing stare issued a cease and desist warning. No way was he going to enrage my best paying client. Not before the ink dried on the cheque. Luckily, he took the hint and bit his lip. I swear I saw a bead of blood form. Tough. I was the boss and piercing stares were there to be obeyed.

"Have you reported his disappearance to the police?"
    Disbelief screwed up her face. "Of course, I have. They say he's an adult and will reappear in his own time."
    "Much as I love the size of your cheque, I'm inclined to agree." I could almost feel those pounds slipping through my fingers.
    "I'll take my custom elsewhere." She half rose from her chair.
    "No so fast. I didn't say I wouldn't look for him."
    No way was I letting that cheque out of my sticky wee mitts.
    "Have you any clue at all where he might be?"
    "If I did, would I be sitting here. Are you for real. I've a missing husband. A son who's distraught about his

toy. And a stepdaughter with her arm in a sling."

She shifted the sleeping boy in her arms, and carried on, "Do I look like a woman who has a clue?"

The accent had slipped again.

Time for a new tactic. "Can you give me the name of some of the gentlemen who were involved in the fracas?"

"They're no gentlemen."

Despite her obvious distaste for her husband's friends she divvied up the names. Addresses eluded her.

She said, "Roderic kept those sorts of things to himself."

I didn't think this was a marriage made in heaven. More one made in pound signs and ignoring the obvious. Why, I don't know. Lady Lucy didn't give me the impression of being thick.

She wasn't quite sure of all his haunts but did pony up some surprising ones. Well, I never. The Laird was a dark horse. Maybe he'd been horsenapped.

Lady Lamont, wearied of giving me information, tucked her son up in his pram and headed for the door. He still wore the nappy and nothing else. I wondered if her huge Gucci handbag held clothes for the boy. Designer clothes no less. Maybe her largesse with the money only stretched as far as herself. I didn't see it, as she seemed to genuinely love her offspring. I wondered how long it would take for a new nanny to appear. Talking of Nannies.

"Hang on. I need the forwarding address for your Nanny."

"What are you talking about?"

"Your Nanny. I need to speak to her."

"As she's only taking a week's holiday it shouldn't be too hard."

"What? I thought you said she'd been sacked."

"Has it escaped your notice that no one is sacked in our household? Clint still clings on to his odious position, and the Nanny is keeping out of the way."

I made a valiant effort not to roll my eyes and sigh. The thought of my bank account helped me contain the darker emotions.

"Have you got a phone number for her."

Her look said pity. Obviously thinking I wasn't quite right in the head, she pulled out her phone and rattled it off.

"Could you repeat that?"

With a weary look she did so. Slowly.

"She'll have no clue where my husband is."

It was my turn for the 'are you addled' look. "I'm still searching for the teddy as well."

At the word Teddy, Theo's eyes opened and he started with the wailing again. I ushered him and his mother out the door. Noisy weans were a regular occurrence in the Claymore senior house, and I knew they would ultimately lead to migraine.

I didn't have time for that. I'd a nanny to speak to.

42

As a woman was involved, I decided Quill needed to come along to the meeting. He could charm the words out of a stoic. This meant the mutt coming too. I also had a suspiciously quiet nephew to care for. Granddad was spending a day on the Golf Course, which I think translated to the clubhouse. If memory served his rounds employed more alcohol than golf clubs. This meant the absence of a car.

Quill, of course, was delighted. He got all excited about the motorbike.

"I could phone someone to take Eagal and the boy."

I remained resolute. His someone might lead the pup into areas that bordered on the outskirts of legal. Despite his tendency to disaster, I quite liked my canine companion. His appearing in a photo, that involved a number on his chest, didn't sit well with me.

It turned out the nanny was taking in the sights and sounds of St Andrews for the week, so we took the bus. She agreed to meet us in a local café as long as we paid for her lunch. Since when did being a PI stretch to providing free meals? She probably earned more in a day than I did in a year; Still, I needed her input in the missing Teddy stakes. She might even have some insight into the missing Laird. Servants know more than anyone ever gives them credit for. According to Hercule Poirot that is. I always felt the detective was a wise man.

When I found out the price of the bus fare I wondered how much a sidecar for the bike would cost. Eagal could sit in there. The picture of him in driving goggles made me laugh out loud, drawing dirty looks from the scowling natives. I wondered what they had to be in such a bad mood about. St Andrews is a bonnie wee place and didn't deserve that level of derision.

The local bus to St Andrews will never be the same again. Eagal, rather than sitting immobile or snoring under the seat like any normal dog, decided to do a recce. This involved him searching in any bag he came across. In his search, he unearthed a picnic, destined for a day at the beach with an old lady and her grandson. By the time I reached him, he'd demolished five sandwiches, two packets of crisps, including the wrappers and a slice of carrot cake.

I slipped the woman a £20 note to replace the lunch and dragged the canine horror back to my seat. Quill, in the meantime, sat angelically gazing out of the window. His approach - disown us. I felt like disowning myself as well. Or at least the blasted dog. The only thing that stood between him being chucked off the bus and me keeping him, was the fact that my father would disown me. Reliant on the bank of mum and dad, no way was I taking any chances.

Somewhere on the outskirts of St Andrews, Eagal parted company with his impromptu lunch. All over the floor of the bus. The obviously newly cleaned floor of the bus. At this point I got up, rang the bell, and jumped off at the next stop. Quill and Hezzie hurtled after me. We'd walk the rest of the way. Coward? You bet. I had to return to Dundee and being barred from Stagecoach was not on my list of things to do today.

The café was lovely, and accepted pets. They even gave the mutt a bowl of water. The waitress sneaked him a small morsel of fruit cake as well. I saw the inches creep o. with every calorie. Serves him right. Hezzie, in seventh heaven, devoured the extra cream cake the waitress slipped him. This kept him quiet throughout the entire conversation.

The Nanny hailed from Germany, here to learn English. I'm not quite sure why as her English sounded perfect to me. I had forgotten any German ever learnt at school. Our teacher was more interested in waxing lyrical over the maths teacher to teach us language skills. We did, however, have a firm grasp of the maths teacher's rippling muscles. In a purely literary sense of course. None of us went anywhere near his muscles in reality, although I did have my doubts about Mimosa. She was interested in anyone wearing a pair of trousers. More certain were the moral standards of the teacher, an upright young man. Yes, I know I'm digressing again.

Despite interrogating Helga, practically to the point of torture, we got no information on the missing Bart. Even bribing her with a rather fine apple strudel didn't work. Although she did admire the strudel, saying it reminded her of home.

"My dear lady what a delightful accent you have." Quill dialled up the charm knob to one thousand.

"My English, it is not good."

"It is a pleasure to make your acquaintance. I have always found German women so insightful and intelligent. You must have some information for this delightful lady."

He waved an expansive arm at me. Well as expansive as a dwarf could manage.

"If I knew something then I would be telling such a gentleman as you."

This went on for several minutes making me want to crawl into a hole and hide. I swear Lexi was going to be fed to the dog for getting me into this.

Even Quill's charms let us down for once. Much simpering, coy smiles and schmoozing, but not one jot of information. Not even a tiny squeak of information. Bother.

Either she was a tough nut to crack, or she knew nothing. My money fell squarely on the latter. She'd have fessed up to Quill in a nanosecond.

She swore Bart was clutched in Theo's hand when she tucked him up in the cot and had vanished when he awoke in the morning. Vamoosed. Gone. Disappeared. Any adjective one could muster. Still no Bart. What?

Closer questioning elicited the toddler claimed escape artist status when it came to climbing from his cot. However, he was confined to the nursery suite and couldn't get out of there if he took the fancy. She remained firm, and I saw her point. The solid wood doors in the family pile didn't lend themselves to opening by a two-year-old. Even one with the skills of Houdini.

This led me to the conclusion it was an inside job. Who in the castle would steal a Teddy from a sleeping toddler?

My money was on Clint, a hoodlum if I'd ever seen one. Plus, he had a mean streak and hated Lady Lucy. I'm sure his general animosity towards the world spread to blonde haired cherubs, possibly even cats and dogs. I might just let Eagal have at him and fail to mount a rescue.

So, I now had an American hoodlum to interrogate.

It was time to dispense with both Quill and the doggie disaster area. Hezzie as well.

This one required solitude. Hi Ho Eagal, Silver not being available.

43

I phoned Auntie Morag and gave her instructions to attend to her mop wielding duties. I wanted the office to smell sweet as a daisy. Penury might be beckoning, but that was no excuse for slipping standards. Also, hint of ammonia is not the perfume which nets the best results in client retention. Certainly not in the PI Business.

It turned out we hadn't been banned from the local buses. God only knows why. Our return to Bonnie Dundee was uneventful. All the scarfing and throwing up had left the mongrel docile so he snored through the journey.

The only minor mishap was when a teenager tripped over his tail and the teen and his dignity went flying. Served him right. Too busy looking at his mobile phone to worry about misplaced tails. I threw him a dirty look and tucked Eagal's tail underneath him. The stupid mutt hadn't even noticed. I swear he was really brain dead and functioning on automatic pilot.

Aunty Morag was in full swing with a bottle of Clorox when we arrived. I ordered Quill on dog walking and nephew watch and headed for the garage. Maybe Hezzie and Eagal were a trifle too much for one diminutive man to handle, but I didn't care. I also didn't care that I was leaving my nephew to the tender ministrations of an ex-con. Quill seemed like a jolly nice bloke, despite his past. My instinct told me he'd do nothing more than teach the lad some breaking and entering. Hezzie being hell on earth already, what did one more misdemeanour matter.

I ignored the fact the Rev Percy might think otherwise.

In the immortal words, I wanted to be alone. More thinking time, and PI's should work alone anyway. I'm not sure how I ended up with an office full of staff. They merely cluttered the place up and cost money. Used to living in the zone whilst working with partners, this ragtag set of misfits was way beyond my abilities or understanding.

Half way to the garage I worked out the first little flaw in my plan. Where exactly was Clint? Maybe he'd vamoosed back to the states. Who to ask eluded me. Dundee might be small, but Aberdeen is humungous. Okay, in Scottish terms. I couldn't just ask random strangers if they knew Clint.

Plus, the day was fast marching on and even conscientious PI's need some time off. I turned tail and headed back to the place from whence I came. It appeared gloriously cleaner, dog and assistant free. Sitting down I drew up a game plan.

Plans don't come in a six pack from Sainsbury. So, it proved trickier than I thought. What I knew about Clint could be written on the back of one of Theo's tiny hands.

I didn't need to be a veteran hacker to find out about the man. Privacy issues didn't bother him as he was all over the internet, large as life and half a dozen times uglier.

Turns out I was right. A Stetson and Oakley's did feature heavily in his wardrobe. He had a wife and a couple of weans, bafflingly left behind in The States. I couldn't figure out if they were estranged or he'd just conveniently left them to their own devices. Maybe they'd waved him off with a chirpy smile and a feeling of great relief.

His scowl appeared to be a permanent fixture. Thank God. Made me feel less threatened if he was merely a miserable sod, not especially keen on offing me.

Turning my thoughts away from my elimination and back to the investigation, I scrolled and clicked for a good half hour. Then boredom set in. The man wasn't only an open book but the dullest one in the library. Or was he? I had this nagging feeling there might be more to him than met the social media eye. I pondered this. A thug. Not overly bright. Did he have enough of the wherewithal or cojones to create a false persona?

All this thinking did nothing more than give me a headache and make me hungry. It was time to head in the direction of my tea.

My motley crew of assistants hadn't checked in. I considered ringing the police. On the other hand, asking if they'd seen a dwarf, a shaggy rug and a demon might find me carted off to the funny farm. Or at least a bollocking from Lachie, for letting them loose on an unsuspecting public. I wouldn't be surprised if they were already tapping the boards in front of some high-ranking police official's office.

Then discretion took over. I rang Quill. The stars in the heavens were obviously aligned as he answered.

"I am, at this precise moment, taking them to your mother's. Young Hezekiah informs me she is an excellent cook and there will be food on offer for everyone."

"No! Wait!"

"We will see you there, young woman. You need to eat more."

With that he cut me off.

Heavens above. Time for a quick detour to the family pile. I ran in the direction of the bike, speed dialling my assistant every two minutes. The swine didn't answer. I swore he was going to swing.

I hadn't got around to telling anyone in the family about Quill's previous employment. My mother would find it extremely entertaining. Not.

Her Wild Indian, or Women's Institute as they prefer to be called, friends would have a field day with that one. I'd been the talk of the town since I wore my first tutu. This little matter took it to a whole nother level and my mother was a right snob on the QT. Me being linked to cons and gangsters would not a happy Mamah make.

Lachie would pin him to a wall and interrogate him using suitable amounts of torture where necessary. My father might, just might, employ one of his antique guns.

44

Despite the bike, I failed to head them off at the pass. By the time I approached the table Quill was chowing down with the family.

All appeared calm. I, on the other hand, was a bundle of nerves and upset stomach. Ballet was a cinch compared to all this drama.

Quill held court with a long and, from the screams of laughter, entertaining tale.

"...and then I said—"

I interrupted. "What are you doing here?"

"Cassandra Claymore, I raised you better than that."

As well as raising me, Mamah also raised an eyebrow that bristled with annoyance. Said eyebrow was never a good sign. It usually meant a trip to my bedroom and a grounding. Thankfully we were long past those days.

"Grab yourself some food and join us."

Politeness tinged with a hint of steel. Oh boy. I was in serious trouble.

"Sit, down girl. We're all starving here." My father shovelled in a forkful of salmon.

I sidled up to Quill, whispered in his ear, and headed for the kitchen.

That should cool his jets whilst I was gone.

The remainder of the evening went as well as could be expected. I was living on my last nerve.

Quill had every lady in the place enthralled, entertained and lapping up his every word. I didn't know if the nauseous feeling in my stomach was due to anxiety or his behaviour.

Everyone else looked gripped by his manners. I
wanted to slap him. In fact, I often wanted to slap him.
For someone who didn't have a malicious bone in her
body, I was turning into some sort of harpy.

Drifting into a reverie, using the time to ponder my case
and my career, I re-entered the room to Elgin saying,
"Keep away from that one. He's a right barstool."
"Bar steward, Grandad. The saying's bar steward."
I thought I ought to make at least a vague effort to
join in the conversation. I soon found out this was a
poor choice of entry point.
"Where do you get off telling *me* off? Remember I
used to dandle you on my knee."
There's no arguing with that.
"You're a Professional Investigator. Go investigate
and stop picking me up for every wee transgression."
Grumpy old so and so. Not that I said that. My father
would ground me for a month no matter what my age.

"Who are we talking about?"
Quill filled me in. It was some joint acquaintance that
everyone, but me, knew. My sojourn in London had me
out of the loop. Another example of my total inability
to give this PI lark a serious go. If they'd put out a call
for the person least likely to go into the detective
business, my name would be at the top of the pile.

With regards to the common acquaintance, I couldn't
figure out why he was a right barstool and didn't have
the energy to figure it out. I had enough of Quill's
mates kicking around without adding another one into
the mix. As long as it wasn't Nutjob Norm it was fine.

I'd no sooner had this thought than an ice-cold felling
raced down my spine.

"We're not talking about your mate Norm, are we?"
"Of course not, dear lady…"

Simultaneously rattled and relieved I stopped listening. I also let the dear lady remark slide. All this worrying about every little utterance was becoming a tad wearing. It also deflected from the real business of finding crooks. If they were crooks that is. So far all I had to find was an auld teddy and a man who nobody actually cared was missing.

Apart from his viper of a sister that is. Most of Dundee wished she were also missing. It remained open to debate whether Florian was clueless or crook. As thick as a cheese scone and a lot less useful – a given if you knew the lad.

After a full nosh, Percy still hadn't appeared, but two or three of her offspring were charging around. The more rambunctious ones. The delightful Phoebe was absent from the scene. Shame.

Judicious questioning elicited the fact Persephone was in the throes of delivering her next sproglet.

"What number is this?" I asked.

My mother drew in a sharp breath. Dear old daddy leapt to my defence. "The lassie has a point. Percy does tend to shoot them out regularly."

An icy stare had my father head down, eating, and looking chastised. Mamah could quell a whirling dervish.

"This is Persephone's sixth for anyone unable to count."

She informed us the girls were with friends. Percy had dumped the kids with anyone who had a pulse. Hence my ending up with Hezzie, the most lively of the lot of them. No one else would take him.

Having had enough food and scintillating conversation I announced my imminent departure. As the shaggy skulked around I needed a car. Elgin offered his. Less largesse and more alcohol driven, I was still keen to accept. Never look a gift car in the bonnet, even if it is a rust bucket.

Quill begged a ride home. Much as I would have left him to walk, I'm a well brought up young woman and Mamah was watching. An agreement of the 'I would deliver him straight to his door' type was therefore struck. Yet again I questioned my suitability as anyone's boss.

45

I still hadn't figured out where my assistant lived. I excelled at picking him up from random places, and spectacularly failed to return him home. Ever I could also lose myself going to the end of a cul-de-sac, so I needed directions.

We were tootling along in blessed silence when Quill said, "I've lost my bearings."

Slightly puzzled as to the turn of the conversation I said, "You told me. Your wee boy's in the states."

"My dear Cassandra, I would value a clue as to why you think it's important to discuss the matter of my son at this particular moment."

The sun had addled his brain. He'd brought the flaming topic up. I gripped the steering wheel hard and managed to keep my tone civil. "You said you'd lost your bairns. I thought you only had one though. How many others are kicking about? It might be useful to tell me about them all."

Even with his stature, his laughter shook the car.

"B-E-A-R-I-N-G-S. I said bearings."

"You should speak English then." The petulant tone in my voice surprised even me.

"On the contrary. I feel *you* should undertake a hearing test."

That was it. I slammed on the brakes and the car burned rubber as it screeched to a halt. I fancied I smelled smoke.

"Out."

"Cassa—"

"What part of the word out didn't you understand? You are so fired you'll end up in Wick."

His movements slow he opened the door. Looked back at me. I remained firm. He jumped down from the seat and gently shut the door.

I left him standing in the road with nary a backward glance or a pang of guilt. I'd had enough.

Three minutes down the road guilt pangs kicked in harder than a stampeding herd of rogue elephants. In case you are wondering, I do know what that is like. My dancing career took me to Kenya, and the opportunity for a Safari was a temptation too far. My personal close encounter with the aforementioned pachyderms had me rethinking future holiday choices. At least in my new occupation, the nearest I'd get to an elephant would be Edinburgh Zoo, and then a chain link fence would keep me safe.

Anyway, I digress. I did a quick U-turn resulting in Quill jumping back in the car and buckling up. Silence resumed apart from the odd turn left, turn right. I deposited him in front of a beautifully maintained set of flats near the Frigate Unicorn. This wasn't where I picked him up when we had our jaunt to the duck and dagger. He could have walked to the flaming pub from here. It was about three minutes away.

"Do you actually live here?"

"I am now domiciled here, and the delightful Lexi is fully aware of my living arrangements."

I suppressed the sudden urge to rip the man's tongue out. With my bare fists. Suspicion still bubbled inside my brain.

"How can an ex-con afford a gaff like this?"

"You grow more like a penny dreadful every day, Cassandra."

I took a deep breath. Then another. Arrest for murder was not in my plans this evening.

"Answer!"

The meaning of hissed through their teeth became suddenly apparent.

"I'm a man of independent means." With that, he sailed serenely off through the door of the building leaving me with a face like a stunned mullet. Quill 1 – Cassandra 0.

46

I'd just about recovered from that shock when another jumped up and smacked me in the face.

Eagal charged up the stairs ahead of me. As I approached, a figure struggled out from under him. Willow thin and growing like a weed, she wore multicoloured shorts and a mustard t-shirt emblazoned with 'Free Tibet'. My sister's surprise package.

"Hi, Aunty Cass." The voice was cheery, young and unexpected. No mistaking my sister Jacinta's daughter, Hebe.

"Where's your mother?" I peered around as though this would assist her appearance. Experience told me this would not happen.

"Still in Peru. She wants me to go to school in Scotland. I'm to stay with you."

"You can't flaming stay with me. You're fifteen for goodness sake. What am I expected to do with a fifteen-year-old?"

I unlocked the door as I spoke.

Hebe followed me in.

"Too late, I'm here with a label round my neck and a jar of marmalade in my hand." There was a thump as the girl threw her rucksack on the floor.

"I'm starved. They give you barely anything to eat on *Cheap as Chips Air*."

She stalked over to the fridge and opened it. Her eyes widened in shock.

"What do you live on?"

Not having seen her for a couple of years she was slightly hazy in my mind. I did remember, however, her legendary ability to put away mountains of food. She hadn't changed much.

"How did you get here? Is there a reason you didn't call?"

"Flights times three. Tram. Train. Walked. No mobile phone. Mum said you'd buy me one when. I arrived."

"How long did it take you to get here?"

"Three days."

I couldn't believe any airline, or any mother, would allow a fifteen-year-old to kick around the world unattended for three days. Thank goodness Hebe is sensible to a fault.

"Give me your mother's mobile phone number?"

I don't know why I bothered as I knew the answer the minute the words came out my mouth.

"Not got one."

The child sounded remarkably cheery for someone who had been abandoned by her mother. I suppose with Jacinta as a mother you needed to be resilient. And adaptable. And independent.

What on earth was I going to do with her? I could barely look after myself.

"One night and you're going to your gran's."

"Does she have food?"

"More than you can ever dream of."

The girl perked right up.

I grabbed my keys and stuffed some cash in my pocket. "Come on. We're off for a bike ride and some Indian."

"Cool. How come you've a spare bike?"

"This one involves a rider, a pillion passenger and an

engine."

"Increíble."

Using my limited Spanish, I took this to mean she approved. Either that or she was cursing. I was willing to give her the benefit of the doubt. Jacinta doesn't tolerate cussing and even with oceans between them, no one messes with Jacinta. She was probably in Peru to commune with her Amazonian ancestors.

We come from a long line of tough women both Dundonian and Russian. My sister took it to a whole new stratosphere.

The canine health and safety hazard got left behind. He didn't like Indian.

The evening went well. Hebe entertained me with screamingly funny tales of her travels, whilst shovelling down enough food for the aforementioned pachyderms. I know teenagers can eat, but this took it to heights hitherto unknown. I nibbled a vegetable Korma and meekly handed over the larger part of my Peshwari nan at the girl's request.

Two words – Mum's food. I was stuffed to the Gunwales with barely a crack in which to allow more food into my stomach.

The sleeping arrangements served to reinforce the urgent need for an alternative place in which to doss. There only being one bed, it was in with me or the sofa. She chose the latter. It appeared pyjamas weren't in her wardrobe, so I chucked a pair of mine at her. Being somewhat shorter and skinnier than me, they drowned her. Still, she had to wear something. A toothbrush had made its way from Peru. Fabulous, as there weren't any of those kicking around spare.

Eagal decided to join my niece on the sofa. I left them to argue the toss as to who had the larger share. I wouldn't put my money on either of them as it was about even on who would be the victor.

I climbed into bed and settled down. Then I bolted back up again.

A crack that would put the Grand Canyon to shame had appeared on the bedroom wall. I swear I saw a couple of constellations through it.

This was all I needed. I still had some savings, but they were dwindling fast. Less like a nest egg and more like a mini egg. I could practically hear the builder's yard till go 'ka-ching'.

I wondered how much money mum and dad had in their bank account.

Then I wondered how much cold hard cash Quill had in his. I was betting he had enough to sort my new abode out and get it in habitable order.

I finished my wondering with how I could approach the matter in the morning.

Too restless to sleep I opened a book and started reading.

'I awoke, lying next to a man in my son's tree house, covered in blood and with no memory of the last 24 hours. The man was alive and breathing and I saw no blood on him, but I could see *all* of him. Kathy Fetterolf stood by the wall, staring. She on the contrary, was covered in blood. Whether hers or mine, I could not tell.'

Cracking start. I snuggled down and carried on reading. Despite the gripping nature of my literary choice, I was asleep by page three and dreaming of bodies dripping in blood, falling out of giant cracks in walls. Not the ideal reading matter for a restful night. The next day, I vowed to go to the library and check out something less violent.

47

The next morning Hebe decided she'd prefer to stay with me. Goodness only knows why as a veggie shake or cold curry was the only breakfast available.

She opted for the curry. Heated in a saucepan. The smell made me slightly queasy, but Hebe's a woman of the world and curry for breakfast was normal for her. In fact, I'd bet one of Lady Lucy's cheques on the certainty her mother fed her like this as a toddler.

I downed a Swiss chard shake. Packed with apples, peaches, avocado and ginger it gets the blood zinging round your body and kickstarts the old brain. I needed as much energy as I could muster.

I remained resolute. She was going to her grandparents' house. No arguments. She did, however, come with me to the office. I couldn't get hold of either of my parents and Hebe has a healthy dollop of Jacinta in her DNA. If I left her to her own devices she'd end up in Norway, or somewhere even more far-flung. I resolved to tie her down for the day.

The phone rang. Percy informing me she had another son, Enoch. The name means dedicated or trained in Hebrew. I hope she made a better fist of training this wee sprite than she did Hezzie. Two of those might just tip Dundee over the edge. Hezekiah means God has strengthened. He certainly had in Hezzie's case. He had the strength of forty other boys and a few girls.

Appropriate congratulatory noises were made. Before I hung up I promised to pop in and see the new arrival.

Arriving at the office, I instructed my surprise package to make coffee. She might as well come in useful and I know her mother would have taught her well. Eagal loved her and followed her into the kitchen. I contemplated the day ahead and what I could do to move things forward.

Pondering the legality of leaving a fifteen-year-old to answer phones in a Private Detective Agency, I called on the Oracle – Google. Turns out it was not only acceptable but legal. Slave labour then.

Quill's arrival once more heralded in a Kafkaesque feel to the place.

"There's a giant rubber duck causing havoc on the way into town."

I opened the drawer and checked the bottle of brandy in my desk. Still full.

"Have you been on the sherbert?"

"No, really. It's an inflatable. They seem to be moving it somewhere."

I'd long known Dundee was a touch on the eccentric side, but this took it to new heights.

"How ginormous?"

"About twenty-five foot I'd say. Not that I'm the person to be asking about height, know what I mean?"

He had a point. Still, giant rubber ducks were extraordinary, even for Dundee, and I intended to get to the bottom of the matter. It would give me something to sharpen my investigator claws on. Yep, not exactly on the trail of Jack the Ripper, but a girl has to start somewhere.

A few clicks of the mouse and it turned out there wasn't much investigating or sharpening needed. Photos of

Donny the Duck were all over social media. A new car showroom was using inflatable animals for its grand opening. I kid you not. A day in the life of a Dundee PI.

I'm not entirely sure what ducks have to do with cars, but who am I to judge. It would appear a monkey and a panda also featured. If nothing else, they would give a slightly festive feel to the occasion. Sometimes Dundee surprises me and not in a bad way.

Still, it was the first case I'd solved so I gave myself a mental high five. One down, and two more serious and well-paid ones to go. It was more important I solved those than worried about inflatable animals.

Hebe appeared, like the goddess she was named after, and dispensed coffee and milk. Smooth and rich it soothed the palette and slipped down the throat like aromatic nectar.

"Where did this come from?"

"Machu Pichu via my rucksack."

Much as I loved my niece, this extra package was almost nicer than the original. My sister knew me well.

Whilst Quill and Hebe got acquainted, I made a few phone calls re the location of our Clint. As I thought, this did not prove to be an easy task. Especially since hoodlums don't pony up the skinny at the sound of a tinkling voice. I needed to work on my 'six packs of smokes a day' voice.

Deciding Hebe might as well come in useful I gave her thirty quid and sent her to buy a couple of gifts for Enoch. One from her and one from me. She set off happily enough, in the direction of town. Given her bohemian lifestyle, I Didn't like to imagine what she might come back with.

Maybe I should have been a lot more specific on what

I wanted. I picked up my phone to ring her then put it down again. Damn. She didn't have one.

48

After phone call twenty-three I decided Quill should take over. He knew more bad guys than me and I'd run out of good guys. Short of pinning down our Roderic and torturing the information from his clenched jaws, I'd run out of ideas.

I gave Quill his instructions, adding, "Stay on the safe side of the law."

"Copy that."

"What have I told you about mimicking the worst in American television. I could arrange to have you deported there. I'm sure your son would be delighted."

"You do have a somewhat short fuse, Cass—"

My short fuse blew right up in his well-moistured face. I swear his beard was singed. After that, he merely picked up the phone and started ringing round.

Hebe returned with the gifts for wee Enoch. She'd done a grand job. Rather than the more avant-garde stores the wee darling headed for M&S sale. As she didn't know the wean's size she'd sensibly bought 3-6 month sized Babygros. Also, some shorts and a tee shirt saying, 'I love my Aunt'.

"Hebe, you're a right wee cracker."

I hugged her. She, being a Claymore through and through, hugged me right back.

Kicking off my shoes I performed a couple of soubresauts and a grand jete. Hebe joined in and we performed a few more moves. I'd forgotten just how good she was. Not quite Royal Ballet material, but then she's never had much time to practice, being dragged around the world.

It loosened me up, but the tension behind my eyes refused to disappear. I slumped down in my chair and put my head in my hands.

"What's up?"

Hebe slumped down in the chair in front of my desk

"I thought you were feisty?"

"My fiest packed its bag and took off with narry a backward glance."

I took in her posture and added, "Sit up straight young lady."

Groaning she did as she was told. Fifteen years of Jacinta taught her it was easier to comply.

Twenty-six years with my mother had taught me to do the same.

Quill finished his phone calls, wandered over and handed me a piece of paper.

I looked at it. Three addresses and another for an upmarket wine bar.

"The gentleman you would like to speak to frequents the establishment most lunchtimes."

"For heaven's sake man, cut to the chase and stop with all the long words."

"He goes for a pint in the Grape and Grain around noon every day. They serve a nice charcuterie—"

"Fine." I pushed my chair back and stood. "I don't need their entire menu."

I picked up my mug and swallowed the remainder of my coffee. Cold, I was tempted to spit it out. Decorum won out.

"I'm off up to Aberdeen. Mind the fort and the brat."

My good-natured niece grinned. She'd been called worse than that.

"You may need assistance. I should come with you."

"Not on your nelly. I'm not leaving a fifteen-year-old in charge."

I took in his expression.

"Grandaddy won't get here in time so you're staying put."

"But—"

"Suck it up buttercup."

I left a stricken Quill, and a laughing Hebe behind, and sauntered to the door. Revenge is sweet.

He still hadn't told me where he was the other day. A mixture of curiosity and peevishness encouraged my mean streak.

49

The trip to Aberdeen now being as familiar as a trip to Tesco, I soon gamboled up the high street with gay abandon. That roughly means I was hurrying to the wine bar. Quill's loquaciousness was quite clearly catching.

A stunningly beautiful woman loitered outside one of the other wine bars. Primped, preened and perfectly presented, she was what my Greek scholar mother would call hetaerae. A high-class companion for a man with money on the hip. To the rest of us, she was an upmarket prostitute.

To prove my point an elderly man in an Armani suit tottered out from the door and took her arm. Her sizzling smile in his direction almost blinded me.

My experience of the city continued as quickly as my walk. One large lady in a velour jogging suit nearly finished me off. She bent over and rummaged in her shopping bag, thus exposing an expansive area of her large derriere. It was more than one woman should ever have to take. Having a couple of hurdies flashed at you of a morning does not get the day off to the best of starts.

I managed to get to the Grape and Grain in good time. The heat and the leathers had my mouth begging for a glass of chilled Krug. I pacified it with a sparkling mineral water.

Not quite the same, but it was too early to be toping.

Plus, my days of sipping expensive champagne are long gone, along with my Royal Ballet pay packet. The pulp fiction detectives drank what they wanted, but they didn't have Police Scotland and their very sensible drinking laws to contend with.

The champagne substitute and I mosied around the place. Clint was indeed in residence, tucked up in a booth at the back, cosied up to what only could be described as a stunner.

I sidled up to him. "How's the wife?"

He turned his eyes away from the stunner's cleavage and looked me up and down. I obviously didn't make the grade, as he looked like he'd swallowed something noxious.

Stunner chipped in. "He's left his wife."

Yeh, right. I'd heard that one before.

I turned to his companion. Looks to me like he's still very much with his wife. I've spent the last few hours looking him up on every social media site known. I can assure you his wife is not aware of her ex status. If that is indeed the case.

Turning back to Clint, I Pulled out my phone.

"Shall we give her a ring just so we're all clear on your current marital status?"

Clint leapt to his feet and glowered down at me. Grabbing my arm, he dragged me across the bar.

"Listen here, Dumbass, get your big mouth out of my business. In fact, take it right out of Aberdeen."

"Big guy, aren't you. Manhandling a defenceless woman."

I said this loud enough that several patrons could hear, without causing a big stooshie. My mother would say I was making a right show of her if I made too much of a rumpus.

"Kindly remove your hands or my ballet training might just come in useful."

I lowered my voice for this part. Didn't want the whole bar to hear me threaten him.

His face adopted the blank look. This bloke would be out of his depth in a car park puddle.

I filled him in. "A petit jeté might just cause you a lot of pain when I kick you right in the cojones.

His look still clueless, he understood enough to cover said cojones with his hands.

"One of my ballet moves might mean your crown jewels suddenly look a tad tarnished." I thought explaining might just be required. And he called me a dumbass.

If nothing else, protection of his prized possessions meant he was no longer clinging to my arm.

"No need for all this animosity," I said, in a soothing voice. "Can I buy you a drink and I'll ask you a few questions?"

He glared at me.

"Then I'll be on my way."

He pushed his Stetson back with one finger. Obviously been watching too many bad movies and was unconsciously parodying. Either that or cowboys really did do that.

Whatever, he still said, "You've got five minutes, little lady."

He dropped down into a chair, indicating I'd be waiting on him.

"I'll have a Coors."

How original. Not. Definitely going with parody then.
What was it with all the men involved in Lord

Roderic Lamont's affairs? They all seemed to be high on testosterone and proving how manly they were. Men were men, and women should know their place. Waiting on men seemed to be the default place.

My fingers itched with the desire to teach him another lesson about women. Only the thought of damaging my piano playing digits stopped me.

50

Much to my amazement, he was still in position when I returned. My brain told me he and his squeeze would have disappeared into the noonday sun the minute my back turned. I was also surprised she hadn't tottered over on her six-inch Manolo Blahnik's to find out what we were up to. Saying that she probably wasn't the brightest bird in the Mearns area. Bright enough to be making top dollar though. You wouldn't receive much change out of eight hundred quid for those shoes. I wondered, briefly, if Clint doled out the readies for her outfit.

"Tell me about this teddy and I'll leave you in peace."
"Ya'll need to leave that behind."
His pseudo southern drawl mild, his eyes were less so.
"A tad tricky when I've been asked to find it. Aint gonna happen."
Two could play at the accent game. And the eye game. I hoped mine looked terrifying as opposed to terrified. The subtle difference may be apparent, but I'm sure it escaped my brain.

He leaned forwards. So did I.
"Who took the teddy from under Theo's nose? You know more about this than meets the eye."
I leaned in even closer.
"I'm sure your right up to your cliched Stetson in its disappearance."
He slapped my face. Hard.

I grabbed his hand and twisted. Hard.

An eye for an eye and all that. I did possess some of the essential skills required of a PI.

Living in London I'd purchased self-defence lessons. Plus, ballet dancers are a whole heck stronger than their skinny frames indicate. You need muscle, pure muscle, to perform all the unnatural moves required of a principal dancer. Or any dancer. Despite retirement, my daily routine keeps my body in tip-top, extra strong condition. Add to that the mean streak I'd developed, and I'm a match for any Stetson toting, Oakley wearing, cowboy.

Every time I saw him I felt like giggling. All I could think of was the steps song '5.6,7,8.' Plus, this guy really was driving me crazy but not in the way the song implied.

Clint squealed like a wee Jessie. Not much of a hard man now, buckling at the merest hint of attack from a lassie.

"Where's the freaking teddy?"

"I. Don't. Know." The capital letters were apparent.

Something in his eyes told me he knew more. I applied heavier pressure.

The squeal turned to a scream.

A waiter scurried over to see what the rumpus was about. The lad was a practically a toddler. How did he score a job here?

"Foreplay," I informed him. "Best not to ask."

The ten-year-old vamoosed quicker than he arrived, his face beetroot red.

Clint was too busy squirming to inform the lad otherwise.

He broke. I knew adding torture to my PI skillset was a grand idea.

"I grabbed the teddy and took it to Lord Lamont." A couple of tears rolled down his cheek.

Damn, I was good at this.

"From a sleeping baby. Real bad guy stuff."

I eyeballed him.

"Why in the name of the blessed Saint Percy would Roderic want you to steal his adored heir's teddy?"

"It's Lord… Owww."

"Stop being such a big chicken."

"I don't know. I swear I don't know."

The tears started in earnest. This time I believed him so let him go. He and his tears disappeared in the direction of the stunner. She could kiss it all better.

51

This had to be the strangest thing I'd come across. What was dear Roderic doing with an antique teddy? That he already owned? Why steal a teddy from his son and then let the whole world search for it? Even more importantly, why allow his wife to spend a fortune employing me to look for it?

The fact he'd allowed her to employ me, specifically me, made a lot more sense. Dave probably told him I'd never find him. What was so important about this particular teddy that he didn't want anyone finding it?

He hadn't flogged it, as not a shop in the area had it. Unless he'd done, or was doing it, on the web. I dialled Quill and gave him instructions.

"Don't involve your dodgy mates."

"Of course, Cassandra."

My full name was a tad better than Dear Lady, but I still felt like I was being told off by Mamah.

One key fact eluded me. Why was Lady Lucy so keen to find a teddy that her husband had? If he needed it for something why didn't he just fess up and buy little Theo another bear?

Instinctively, I knew the reason why. Because whatever Theo's daddy was doing with the teddy, nefarious purposes were involved as Quill would put it. For once, the loquacious version summed it up beautifully.

My time here was done. Another visit to Castle Lamont

beckoned. I spent more time there than my own wee shack. Despite this, it dawned on me that I didn't actually know the real name of the Lamont family pile.

Some Private Investigator I was turning out to be.

52

This time, I intended to enter by fair means or foul. Amazed at how quickly I was moving from the legal to the slightly less legal, I trotted off for a little scout around. That wouldn't hurt at all.

Stopping beside a small copse, thick with Silver Birch and Aspen, I hauled my wheels inside. Having locked my leather jacket inside the pannier, I went for a nice walk in the country. Just a wee lassie enjoying a summers day. This PI gig seriously rocked.

It started off so well. I wandered round the perimeter, poking into bushes, staring at the wall, and eyeing up trees that could double as a ladder. Idyllic. Enjoyable. Fruitless. I also looked at the various hedgerow flowers, inhaling their scent. All was right with the world.

A loud roaring sound made me jump. I whirled around, eyes wild, as adrenaline shot through my body faster than a clown from a cannon.

The sound came closer. Then closer still.

Before I could take make one fight or flight move, a man came crashing through the undergrowth. As he headed straight in my direction flight won, and I lashed out. Blindly, but still managed to hit my target. Hard.

Unfortunately, I clutched a pair of heavy-duty cable cutters I'd relocated from my dad's garage. 24 mm in case you were wondering. I know this because he'd informed me of every single millimetre in boring graphic detail. Alongside everything I could use them for. This did not include killing people.

The tool made contact with the man's head and he fell like a stone at my feet. What had I done? Kneeling down, yes, I know that was stupid, I felt for a pulse. I'm not sure why as I'd never felt a pulse in my life, but I thought I'd better try. Moving my hand around his neck. I felt nothing. Anywhere.

That was when I darted into the bushes and parted company with that hummus sandwich. I phoned for the police and an ambulance. No use taking any chances with the possible expiry of my victim.

His feet were sticking out into the road. Should I move him out of harm's way. I leaned on a tree and contemplated this deeply. Actually, I was trying to keep upright but the deep and meaningful version sounds better.

In the end, I sat on the verge and waited. Away from the body.

53

The good old NHS came up trumps and came screaming up to me in about fifteen minutes. Ambulance men and police leapt from various vehicles and charged in my direction. I was shoved out of the way in a rather spectacular fashion. This involved me landing on my derriere, in a patch of briar. I yelled and leapt to my feet causing even more of a stooshie as the paramedics and the boys in blue told me to shut it and stand by. Somewhere close. I did their bidding, not wanting to spend time in an Aberdeen police cell. Or any police cell for that matter.

An officer came sauntering up to me. Of all the cops in all the towns, why did it have to be 'bacon'. Scotland's riddled with cops yet I only ever saw this one. Was he stalking me?

"Claymore. What are you doing here?"

'I could have asked him the same. His patch was Dundee, so he'd no right to be sauntering around the wilds of Aberdeenshire.

"Stay where you are and don't move."

The reason for his presence became clear. Persecuting me. They'd already given me that order so no reason for him to stick his oar in.

"Why were you lugging a lethal weapon anyway?"

Ah. So, we came to the real reason. He fancied nicking me for murder, or carrying a lethal weapon, or anything really. His sarge was obviously giving him a hard time over his arrest record.

My befuddled brain dragged itself to attention and

chucked a few answers around.

Beligerance won out. "Fixing the bike."

"That bike looks pretty healthy to me."

"Are you suddenly a motorbike mechanic or something?"

To be honest I couldn't understand why the coppers hadn't immediately arrested me. And the cable cutters. I pretty much told them on the phone what had happened. The cable cutters were also in my hand. It didn't take the brains of a Bishop to work out I'd helped him shuffle off this mortal coil. I sat down again. Abruptly.

This gave me time to think. On the plus side, the missing Florian wasn't missing anymore. On the negative side, Mimosa was not going to be happy I'd erased her brother. She'd be asking for that four thousand quid back. Not that I'd be worrying about that in chokey. Despite my situation, I couldn't help wondering about the coincidence. How come Florian tripped up now? Here? Not a sixpence throw from Lord Lamont's estate. Could the two cases be joined at the hip? I was increasingly convinced the two cases were very much joined at the hip. Siamese twin level attachment in fact.

A sudden thought caused me to rush into the bushes and part with my stomach contents again. There was little left from the first attempt.

One of Florian's so-called mates told me this was going to happen. He'd also said Mimosa was in danger as well. I needed to catch up with her pretty damn quick before her brother's murderer caught up with her.

Unless, of course, I was his murderer. Then the battleaxe'd be in no danger whatsoever.

At the thought that I might have killed someone, I

started to shake. I pulled out my phone to ring Percy. I could use a healthy dose of prayer.

For once Percy was sympathetic, making me realise why her parishioners like her so much. I forbade her to tell mum.

"As you've come to me for spiritual guidance, I can't tell anyone."

Thank God for that. And I meant thank God.

"You'll be fine, Cass. You're a Claymore. For what it's worth, by the sound of what you're saying you didn't kill him."

"How the heck do you know?"

"I've seen a few dead bodies in my time, lovey. I know a thing or two."

You haven't seen this one."

She promised me her best prayers and hung up.

I might not like Mimosa, but that doesn't mean I wouldn't do everything in my power to protect her. The boys in blue needed to know about her future demise.

They might need to know, but that didn't mean they wanted to pay a blind bit of notice to me. It turned out the whole of Scotland hated Mimosa, not just me. Everyone has to be famous for something.

I tried my best, I really did. Every which way in fact. The threat of arrest for obstruction hung heavy over my head if I carried on bothering them. Their words were a tad more explicit, so I'll leave it to your imagination to work it out. I still couldn't figure out why they hadn't yet arrested me for murder. I was my number one suspect never mind theirs.

It transpired they were far too busy doing important forensic things and keeping me out of the way. I stood and waited for them to notice me and take me for an interview. I wondered if this interview would involve a police cell, recording equipment and cutting off my access to decent coffee. I'm not sure which bit of this frightened me the most.

Eventually, they came to take my statement. I was ushered to a police car and driven to a nearby café. Despite Lachie's occupation, the inside of a real police car remained a foreign concept. The kind with blue lights on the roof. The rozzers commandeered it as a temporary HQ. The café, that is. Not the car. The owners were making out like bandits on the sale of drinks and sticky buns.

They bought me a coffee and a slice of cake. The minute the snack hit my stomach it turned rancid. I swallowed. Swallowed again. Decorating a police officer with suddenly re-emerging carrot cake, wouldn't look good on my CV.

They recorded everything and then told me my fate.

I didn't realise I was holding my breath until they spoke.

"You didn't kill him."

They couldn't quite say what had helped him into the afterlife, but they were clear it didn't come about at my hands. Even if those beautiful hands contained a set of cable cutters. The beautiful hands words were his, not mine. I expected better of Police Scotland, but I was willing to forgive any transgression.

I could have kissed the man.

In fact, I did something quite out of the ordinary. I did kiss him. Then, realising what I had done, I sprang back like I'd been electrocuted.

"I'm so sorry. Don't know what came over me."

I did know what had come over me. The man was pretty easy on the eye at the best of times. Relief turned him into Adonis and Cupid all rolled into one gloriously kissable package.

He turned a fetching shade of red and informed me he understood. Quite gallant if you ask me.

"The police surgeon says there's no sign of a wound on his head. From the bruise on his shoulder, you whacked him there." He pointed to the offending area on my shoulder. "Sounds like self-defence if you're to be believed."

I slumped back in the seat, tears pouring down my face.

"You'll have to come to the nearest station for a proper interview. But you're free to go in the meantime."

The queasiness flew out of the window and left me craving sugar. I told the sugar rush to do one and bought a banana. Ballet dancers don't keep balletic by stuffing cake. Although I was willing to wager the adrenaline zinging through my body for the past couple of hours took a few pounds off.

They recorded all my details and told me not to take any long holidays. Away from the immediate area that is. They had to be having a laugh. I was so busy I couldn't afford a day off never mind a holiday. Also, so barasic I could hardly afford the money for petrol to Aberdeen and back. Long sojourns elsewhere were completely out of the question.

I was fast discovering a PI's life is never her own.

54

Elgin was in residence when I finally returned to the fold. This cheered me up as I had a job for him over and above your average office minding duties. No sooner had my proposal left my mouth than the entire situation went south faster than a sailor from a burning ship.

I stared at him wondering what had brought this on. Rather than my meek and mild grandad King Kong had appeared, like an apparition, in the room. Blimey, I thought my suggestion was quite pleasant.

"No way, hen. No. No. No." He paused, then for good effect. "No."

He thought I hadn't got it at the first no.

His face turned putrid. In fact, the colour it was before his last heart attack.

"Keep your skin on. I asked you to look after my allotment. Not fly to Mars."

Along with the Agency and the useless pooch, I'd also inherited an allotment. Goodness only knows what Uncle Will thought I was going to do with that. I couldn't even keep a weed alive. Some sort of management company kept my garden in pristine condition, one of the main reasons for buying the flat.

Grandad's response left me even more baffled.

"*He's* up the allotment."

His mouth snapped shut and he refused to open it again. All my pleading couldn't elicit any further information. Actually, never mind further. Any information at all. What in the name of all that's holy, did this man do to grandad?

My ragtag band of staff were updated on my adventures. Quill and grandad clucked like a pair of demented chooks. Hebe laughed fit to bust the windows.

"Jeez. Being here's much more fun than spending time with Jacinta."

I swore them all to secrecy, under threat of death. I drew the line at giving Hebe a contract. I did blackmail her, however. She still wanted to come with me. I gave in, saying she would be at her grandmother's faster than I could say 'pack up' if she breathed one word to my mother.

On the way home, I added several bars of chocolate to her bribe. Shopping beckoned, and they had a deal on Cadbury's.

Later that night the doorbell rang. Lexi entered, clutching a couple of bottles of an excellent Austrian Riesling. I grabbed Edinburgh Crystal glasses, delaying her bollocking. No use ruining a nice wine with a full-blown row.

In vino veritas. In wine there is truth. It was as good an approach as any I'd already tried. I raised a glass of the dry 'elixir of life' to Pliny the Elder the originator of the phrase. In vino veritas that is, not elixir of life. Oh, you know what I mean. A wise man indeed. I wasn't getting much truth otherwise, so wine was as good an approach as any.

I took a restorative sip and rolled it around my mouth. Beautifully dry with hints of lemon and lime and not too sweet. Just what was needed to soothe the soul. And trust me, after envisaging a lifetime in the slammer, my soul needed soothing.

"How's Quill working out?"

"It's a flaming good job you've kept out of my way." I scowled at her. "He's swinging somewhere between helpful and annoying."

"That's our Quill." She grinned and blew me a kiss.

A bit like Quill, Lexi could charm the birds out of the trees.

"Besides, he's a good chap. He really does want to turn his life around."

"That doesn't mean he has to turn it around with me."

"Stop complaining. You need an assistant and I'm sure his specialist skills will come in very handy."

"I'm not letting his specialist skills anywhere near my business. I'd rather like to stay in that business."

"Wuss."

"Yep."

Talk turned from work to her upcoming wedding. It also turned to the fact I hadn't seen my own cockney fella for a while. He obviously had enough bread to make his own toast, and a cupboard filled with wine and beer. Maybe I should visit him.

55

Blue skies heralded a new, gloriously sunny day. A perfect day for a walk, so I set Hebe and Eagal off on their very own walk to my parents' house. Not filled with confidence in their prompt arrival, I was confident it would happen sometime. They'd both need to feed their habit. Mealtimes would act like a beacon. What mischief could they get up to in Dundee?

It was a long walk to the Ferry, but my niece could cope. Her mother dragged her to Everest Base Camp by the time she was ten. By the tales afterwards, she reached it first and had a curry cooking before the rest of the party arrived. Including the Sherpas. She'd packed more miles into her brief existence than most people do in a lifetime.

The early hour meant the pair wouldn't die of heat exhaustion. Just to make sure I tucked a couple of bottles of water into her backpack. I also made a mental note to buy more water.

My shortcomings as a PI becoming further apparent with every move, I remembered, whilst taking my own stroll to work, I hadn't looked into either Lamont's' backgrounds.

I set Quill onto the Lord and I took Lady Lucy. Easiest search ever done to be honest. The pair of them were splashed around every newspaper in the Kingdom. This got me wondering why it was still called a Kingdom when we had a Queen. Turned out it's because the word

Kingdom is gender neutral. Who knew? You learn all sorts in this game.

Lady Lucy hailed from London town. Might Larbert know her? I dismissed the idea quicker than it flitted through my brain. Dundee, where everyone knows everyone and their business, gives you a false sense of perspective.

She appeared in the limelight when she started dating Lord Lamont. Prior to this, she'd been a WAG of a minor league footballer. They met at a Gala Dinner and the rest they say is history.

I wondered how her boyfriend felt about Roderic snatching her. A quick search showed him to be married to another trophy wife. So, no issues there.

Her maiden name was Black, and she had an unremarkable upbringing. Her IQ, on the other hand, was surprisingly remarkable. A scholarship to a public school led to Oxford where she obtained a first in English Literature. You'd think the woman could investigate her own case, her having more brains than me.

Quill's take on Roderic - born into privilege and then multiplied the family profits in a myriad of different ways. What those ways were, no one could figure out. A lot of innuendo, rumour and good old-fashioned fiction figured largely. He was a thug wrapped up in toff's clothing. Allegedly.

A little free with his fists, his first wife walked off into the sunlight not glancing back. She left her daughter so dear old daddy didn't come after her. How on earth had Fenella grown up to be a fairly normal, well-adjusted teenager? From deductions so far, I think Lucy had a lot to do with that. She did seem to protect the kids from Roderic's worst excesses. And despite her protestations, she appeared to love her stepdaughter like her own.

I couldn't quite figure out why she stayed. The Bratlings and enough money to sink an ocean-going liner were probable cause. I wouldn't stay with someone who's fists spoke first. No for all the money in the world. I did wonder if it was worth tapping him for a loan though. I'm not that proud that I wouldn't take my money where I could acquire it. Then I realized Lord Hoodlum was already financing my lifestyle. In a major way.

How the other half live. Time to look into Roderic's dealings in a more thorough way. This demanded a visit to Lachie.

56

I pointed the nose of my motorbike in the direction of Bell Street station and insisted I speak to my brother. The desk sergeant knew me better than he knew his own kids. He'd seen me more often. It still didn't help me much – Lachie was out on a job. I sat down to wait. It involved slowing my breathing and using my mouth. The lobby was littered with waifs and strays. Packed in fact. Close proximity, long waits and the heat added a certain sour odour to the proceedings.

The sergeant, a discerning man, didn't want a wuss of a ballerina spark out on his station floor. He ushered me through to another room with a stern admonition to sit down. I soon found myself with a huge mug of diesel in my hand. Reliably informed it was coffee, I didn't believe him. It would fall foul of the trades descriptions act. In numerous ways. I looked for a pot plant. None.

Desperate measures were called for. I waited until my babysitter stepped out to do some work and dashed to the open window. My coffee went out, and a scream went up and then flew in. Oh, my giddy aunt. What had I done?

Taking the cowards way out I dashed out the door.
    "Thanks for the coffee, Sarge. I'll be on my…"
    "Cass Claymore. Not so fast."
    Even I had to admit Lachie looked better without the rivulets of brown liquid making their way down his cheek. As far as I could tell most of it had missed his

head but not his hitherto white shirt. Even Mamah would be hard pressed to wash that stain out. In fact, the she-bear was going to make my life hell over that. The words 'show of me' sprang immediately to mind.

Busted.

Why in the name of the good God above did he choose that particular moment to return? He should be out feeling collars.

I thought about making a dash for it. The fact my slender, debonair brother was actually the strongest person this side of Hadrian's Wall, stopped me. His newly stained shirt hid muscles of titanium never mind steel. Experience taught me escape was futile.

Every cloud and all that. The effect of this wee debacle meant I was summarily marched to Lachie's office. Him being a fastidious so and so, he had a spare shirt, which he took off to the nearest bathroom. He returned with wet hair and looking his usual pristine self. He' also calmed down. I could tell this by the fact he was now breathing. My investigative skills were improving by the second.

"Explain yourself?"

I'm not sure if it was a question, a command or both, wrapped up in a couple of terse words. I thought about taking the moral high ground and ignoring him. Then sense stepped in. I needed help.

"That stuff's horrible. How can you call it coffee?" I opted for bravado.

"It's a nick, not the flaming Ritz. Why are you cluttering the place up?" He opted for outrage.

Five minutes of not drawing breath and he had the barest outline of what I needed."

"Is this a joke?"

"No."

"I am not, I repeat not, looking into the affairs of a Lord of the Realm." He stopped. His breathing steadied. "Not on your whim, and not on your nelly."

"Lachie, I swear he's up to something. I just know it."

"Female intuition? Feel it in your waters? Brainstorm? All the above."

He inhaled through his nose. Several times. In and out. Deeply. His mouth opening and closing several times added a certain demented look to his features.

"You grow crazier by the minute, Cassie."

"There's no need to be so cutting. Something's telling me. Honestly."

"Whatever it is, let it go and tell you somewhere else. Preferably in Aberdeen."

"Just a wee peek. If he's not got form, I'll scram."

"Scram anyway. Out of my nick before I arrest you."

"What for? You fancying framing me for something I haven't done? Mamah'll love that."

"Assaulting a police officer."

"You big jessie. It was a trickle of coffee."

At this, his dander rose and catapulted through the ceiling. Dismissed forthwith, and escorted off the premises, I found myself doing a solo dance on the wrong side of Bell Street front door.

To be honest I was a tad fed up of men throwing me out. Where did they think they got off? My brother should know better and I'd a good mind to tell him. On second thoughts, maybe not.

"And don't come back."

I swear if it was possible to slam the door he would have done it. He needed to watch that temperament of his. Old age wasn't doing it any favours.

I picked up what remained of my dignity and sauntered down the street. No way was I showing I was either bothered or ill informed.

57

Having failed with one relative, I tried another. What's the use of having the biggest family in Dundee, heck in Scotland, if you can't make good use of it?

I called Percy.

"I need your guild on the case."

"And you say Grandad's batty? What in the name of the blessed Saint Andrew are you wittering about?"

"Can I borrow your guild women? A bunch of nosy worthies keeping their eyes and ears to the ground is just what I need."

If Percy's voice grew any chillier it could build an igloo. "Cass Claymore..."

"Jump off your high horse, Perce. I haven't got time. I'm coming over."

My new nephew was as cute as. One quick cuddle and my heart melted so fast I could swear a puddle appeared on the floor.

"You're Enoch's Godmother. Or you will be when he's christened. Keep the date free."

I've no clue what date. I was too busy adoring my nephew. Most folks ask if you'd like to be a Godparent. Percy had run out of willing participants, so she was down to recycling relatives. I tried to work out how many Godchildren I had. Six I think. Or it could be seven. With my family, it's difficult to tell.

"What do you want with the Women's Guild?"

I tore my eyes away from Enoch long enough to

answer. Then I thought I'd better hand the sweet-scented bundle back to his mother. It was hard to concentrate when in the midst of adoration.

"I'm having difficulty pinning down the background and current whereabouts on certain Lord Lamont."

"And why should anyone in my church be interested in this?"

"The women in your Guild know more about Scotland's inhabitants than the Government does."

"Your probably right. Still, no way you are getting near them."

"Percy, I'm desperate."

I informed her someone had died, possibly murdered. Actually, I didn't know that yet, but needs must. Us PI's use anything at our disposal to wrest information from our witnesses.

The stalwart Percy, paled.

I had a sudden thought. One even worse than murder. "Don't you dare tell, Mamah. You're under oath, right."

"This isn't a court, you dozy bint. Nor a confessional."

"But you won't tell?"

"You sound a like a two-year-old." Her nose wrinkled.

I'd always wondered what that looked like. Now I knew.

"I've better things to do than tittle-tattle about you."

Now she sounded like a two-year-old. I was transported back to the nursery where she ordered me around like she was running her own personal fiefdom.

"So, can I speak to your ladies?"

"Not a chance."

"When's their next meeting?"

Her eyes narrowed, and a variety of emotions

flickered over her face. Years of reading Percy gave me my answer.

"That'll be now then."

I leapt up and did a little celebratory cabriole. Then I marched in the direction of the church hall.

Cass…"

Years of ignoring the reverend chipped in. I continued marching, she hurried after me.

58

My entrance to the church hall was not balletic perfection. In fact, it was more music hall than classical. Just as I reached the doorway, Percy reached *me*.

Rushing up behind me she made a valiant effort to grab my collar. I performed a quick sidestep, which resulted in Percy continuing her forward momentum – headlong to the floor. Trying to avoid her I tripped over the step and landed in an ungainly heap right on top of the Reverend Percy.

At the commotion, the room went silent. Apart from one of the deafer worthies who carried on singing. What she was singing was anyone's guess. As well as being deaf she was also tone deaf and her tune bore no resemblance to any ever written.

As my sister struggled to her feet and tucked in an errant strand of hair, I knew this would not end well. She'd have me on babysitting duties every day for the rest of my life.

She gathered what was left of her dignity and said, "My idiot sister would like a word with you all. I'll make the tea."

She drifted off in the direction of the kitchen, refastening her dog collar as she went

I was left wondering why I'd got off so lightly. A feeling of dread settled in my stomach making me feel nauseous. What was she planning?

The ladies were delightful and more than willing to answer my questions. As I thought, they knew a lot about the Lord and his family. Turned out he'd always been a brat.

"His mother, delightful lady, spoiled him rotten."

"She did splash the cash a bit though."

"Oooh. Listen to you, Nora. All up to date with your words."

"I've got thirteen teenage granddaughters so—"

"Ladies, the Lord? Roderic I mean. Not the almighty."

Gossip's all very well but I needed the right type.

"As I was saying, his mother spent cash like it came down with every shower."

After an hour of useless babble, three cups of tea and several stale custard creams, I left with no further information. I did, however, have a burning desire to find out where all Roderic's money came from. Sounded like darling mummy had burned through the family coffers pretty fast during her lifetime.

59

By this point, I'd run out of relatives who could in any way help me. I'd also remembered that there were a couple of locked doors, inside the Lamont family pile, that I hadn't investigated. Seriously. Mike Hammer would have been through those doors days ago.

I wondered about asking Lady Lucy what was in there, then manners kicked in. And common sense. The doors were locked for a reason and she wouldn't just usher me through. Even if she had a key, which I very much doubted. She would also be asking stern questions. They type where I'd have to fess up to knowing which doors in her home were locked.

The law-abiding Larbert would never lend me *his* keys. So, I decided it was time to use Quill's specialist skills.

My assistant, giddy with excitement, readily agreed.

"Consider it done, dear lady. Consider it done."

"If you're caught you take the blame. I'll deny all knowledge."

"I wouldn't dream of mentioning you. Why would I drag such a delightful lady into my mess?"

"Tell me nothing. That way I can be quite honest when I deny any involvement."

"My lips are sealed."

I sent him home to prepare and followed suit before I could regret my decision. He'd informed me that he would perform the deed that evening and that I could expect a satisfactory resolution by the morning. A flaming long way to say, I'll do it tonight.

I arrived home to a teenager and a dog. They were inside my flat, along with Larbert. None of them should have been there. It was pointless asking how they'd entered.

Larbert was cooking up a culinary masterpiece, which involved a lot of pineapple and spices.

My niece took up the entire sofa and appeared to be fast asleep. Eagal snored in a cool corner. The perfect picture of family harmony. Only I wasn't married and didn't have a family. Not this type anyway.

I prodded my niece. Then prodded her again. Bleary-eyed, she struggled to an upright position.

"Hi, Auntie Cass."

"Never mind hi, you should be at your gran's."

"I told you, I've decided to stay here. Ded and Angus are coming over later to build a bed."

Ded is Russian for Grandfather. It's what my nieces and nephews call my dad to make it less confusing. Elgin is Grandad. My dad's DIY skills are marginally better than Angus's but not much, so I didn't hold out much hope on the bed front. At least the lass would have a mattress to lie on.

One thing puzzled me more than my niece's sleeping arrangements. The sight was strange. One I certainly didn't expect to see.

An antique bear sat on my coffee table. It looked just like Bart, the missing teddy.

60

Staring is not something expected of a well brought up Dundee lassie. But, stare I did.

"Where did that come from?"

"The doorstep." Hebe had managed to stir herself from her languor long enough to focus.

"I could swear you said the doorstep."

I shook my head in an effort to dislodge the fuzz taking up residence in the space my brain should be occupying.

"I did." A girl of few words.

"Whose doorstep?" I could be equally brief.

"Yours. The one you just stepped over." Hebe looked at me as though I was two dancers short of a corps de ballet.

I was beginning to think I was several dancers short of a corps de ballet. How, in the name of all things Scottish, did Bart end up on my doorstep?

I picked the offending teddy up and informed the collected company we were both leaving.

"The curry will be ready in about an hour." Larbert left his stirring long enough to come over and kiss me in a pleasing manner.

Thoughts of leaving tried to fly from my lips. I gave them a stern telling off and pulled away.

Larbert's thumb caressed my cheek turning my stomach to fire and my brain to jelly. My resolve stayed. I kissed Larbert again, more sister than girlfriend, and prepared to trot off and do investigatory things. Quite what these were, I had no idea.

"Keep the food hot for me." I snaffled a couple of chunks of pineapple.

With that, sweet juice running down my chin, Bart and I took a jaunt to the office.

This investigator lark is more work than it looks. Nevertheless, I was used to dancing every day, with matinees twice a week, so stamina was stamped in my genes. Adding an evening shift to my routine wasn't a hardship.

I unlocked the filing cabinet, yanked open the drawer, and pulled out one of the only two files. It was quite lonely in that drawer.

I'd no sooner opened the filing cabinet than the door clattered open and battered off the wall. What the...?

Mimosa filled the doorframe. I mean literally filled the doorframe. She seemed to have grown even larger since I last saw her.

Her face told me she had a whole basket of bones to pick with me. Maybe if she left most bones alone she'd be svelte. The thought flitted across my mind and made me giggle. I just couldn't help it.

"You killed my brother. Think it's funny, do you?"

I quickly caught hold of myself and adopted a more sombre look.

"I'm sorry for your loss."

"Sorry! Sorry!" Her voice reached a crescendo as she hurtled across the room. "You caused my bloody loss."

I quickly sidestepped as being crushed by a barrage balloon wouldn't be good for my knee.

"No need to shout, this is a respectable area."

Just to prove how respectable the door opened, and a man bolted through. Sporting black shorts, matching t-shirt and a chest the size of china, he looked like a half way well-dressed thug. The thug part came about by the tattoos that covered every inch of exposed skin. Including his head.

"I'll give you shout—"

A meaty hand clapped over Mimosa's mouth effectively silencing her. I silently thanked my knight in tattooed armour as peace descended.

"She giving you trouble, hen?"

As Mimosa struggled in the man's hands my brain caught up. This man looked just like Nutjob Norm himself. Why was he decorating my parquet flooring?

"I wis just passing and heard her screeching. Worse than Senga fae the Gorbals after a wee swallie."

I had to admit his description was a good one. That didn't mean I wanted him in the middle of my case. Especially since 'just passing' around here indicated only one thing. A visit to the top floor loan shark. He probably owned it.

Much as I loved seeing Mimosa squirm, I said, "Leave the poor woman alone."

Norm, if that was who this was, dropped her like a sack of tatties. A well-behaved thug then. She landed on the floor with a screech.

His look said, one more syllable and I'll silence you permanently. My gaze searched his body for any signs of a weapon. None. If his figure-hugging attire was to be believed. We were safe. Unless there was a gun tucked in the back of his shorts. Sneaking close enough to find out, wasn't an option.

"She's had a bereavement. Grieving. I'll take care of her."

With a look that said that they'd be grieving her death, the man disappeared.

He left me wondering what on earth that little display of masculinity and chivalry was all about. Did Quill have him standing bodyguard? I swore I would swing for my assistant, the minute I clapped eyes on him.

My worries weren't over. I still had the madwoman to cope with. This was more burden than any PI ought to bear.

Thankfully, the interlude with Nutjob, or whoever he was, had cooled Mimosa's pipes a bit. Emphasis on the bit. She was still madder than a polecat in summer.

"What did you do to my brother? I asked you to find him. Are you too stupid to know I meant alive?"

The effort being too much for her she plonked herself down in a chair. It creaked but held on manfully. Quality furniture. I'd had a feeling some of my clients may be of the more rotund variety. She did continue to screech.

"If you'd shut up for a minute I'll explain." The loan shark's floor rattled as the sound bounced off it.

Her trap snapped shut and silence reigned. I gloried in it for a few seconds.

"I. Didn't. Kill. Your. Brother."

It took her grieving brain a few seconds to absorb this.

A haunted look came over her face and the sobs started.

I dispensed, tissues, tea and TLC in equal measure. Once she'd recovered, I explained. Only the coroner knows, or will know, how he died. I do know it wasn't me."

"You said you whacked him."

"With a spanner. On the shoulder. That doesn't constitute GBH."

There's no such thing as GBH in Scotland but I didn't

want to befuddle Mimosa's tiny brain with inconsequential matters.

61

Having bundled the grieving sister out of the door, more pressing matters awaited. Time fast marched on and my stomach told me dinner time was long gone. I thought of ringing for a takeaway from menopause mansions but decided against it. The longer I kept my mother at bay, the better.

My new bestie, Bart the Bear, required attention. If that was who he was. I pulled him out of my rucksack. This was Fendi and a hangover from my more affluent days. It used to hold Dom Perignon. Now it was reduced to old teddies.

This specimen certainly looked old enough to be Bart.

I opened the file and compared. Yep. Definitely the same teddy.

He was an ugly looking thing, making me wonder why all the fuss. You'd think the aristocracy could afford a celebratory teddy when a new infant shot out. The stuffing seemed to be pouring from this one.

At least I'd solved my first case. Or had I? Could the fact Bart had appeared on my doorstep count as solving a case? And the much more important question – who dumped him?

I deliberated. Should I investigate further, or tell Lady Lucy I was done. Would Lucinda pay me expenses after I'd actually found her lost property? The answer to this formed my next move. As my hand hovered over the phone my brain took in the lateness of the hour. Tomorrow morning would have to do. A curry was calling my name.

No sooner had I locked the filing cabinet than the shrill ring of a mobile shocked me out of my stupor. Within fifteen seconds of answering all the blood ran to my feet leaving me in no fit state to chat.

62

Sinking to the floor and leaning against the wall I recovered my equilibrium. Quill was on the phone with a tale I didn't want to hear.

"Did you say…" I drew in a deep breath, "Drugs." The weakness in my voice worried even me.

In sharp contrast, Quill sounded far too cheery. "I did. All three rooms are stuffed full of the highly addictive assortment. There's cocaine, marijuana, spice, legal highs ecstasy, uppers downers, all round abouters,.."

"What?"

Okay, I made that last one up. But the rooms are being used as drug larders. All neatly labelled and ready to ship out. Seems our Roderic is maintaining the family pile by dealing."

"Out of there. Now." My voice now trembled and rose a few octaves. It did a nice job in hitting every note ever written.

"Darling girl, I'm halfway to Dundee. Sit tight. I'm coming to see you."

I hung up and picked up Bart, ready to chuck him in my backpack. Then something struck me harder than the drunk driver who took out the old knee. That wasn't stuffing coming out from the tatty bear's seams. Bart the Bear, was actually Bart the Drug Mule.

This was becoming serious. Me harbouring a drug-stuffed bear overnight could land me in the type of trouble that would see me doing time. I contemplated phoning Lachie. Nah. A ten-minute walk to Bell Street, I'd deliver Bart and my findings to them.

Doing my civic duty felt good.

Not wanting a rucksack full of cocaine, I carefully placed Bart in the only thing I could find. A Tesco carrier bag. Strolling up the street I held firmly to the handles and contemplated my situation. Important thoughts occupied my mind.

Would the police arrest me the minute I handed Bart over?

How long would they interrogate me for?

Would they believe me?

Would Lachie go nuts? That one was actually a really good point. Fairly tolerant, this little foray into the world of drug running might just tip him over the edge into insanity.

Would Lady Lucy give me a reference after little Theo's toy and her husband, both ended up in custody?

Would I ever savour my curry?

Deep in thought, I was oblivious to my surroundings. This was not advised by the best PIs whether in a novel or the real McCoy.

The first indication of trouble was when a large hand clamped over my mouth.

The second was when the world went black.

63

I awoke with several jackhammers playing the Radetzky March in my head. I cursed Johann Straus II for ever having written it. Lifting my head proved an almost insurmountable task, but several attempts later I was able to view my surroundings. Bleak!

Actually, they weren't that bleak, but the fact I was *tied* to an otherwise comfortable bed meant they were less palatial than they could have been. A four-poster bed. This did nothing to lift my mood. The last such bed I'd slept in was in a hotel in Paris. No way I was there. More likely Aberdeen. Enjoying the hospitality of a drug-dealing Lord of the Realm.

Despite my plight my fashion conscious, sub-conscious took in the Liberty wallpaper was and Yves Delorme bedding. My snobbish side appears in the most unexpected ways. And the most unhelpful times. God Help me.

My head flopped down again as I considered my situation. My brain felt like someone had been doing experiments on it. How was a girl supposed to think under these circumstances?

"Think. Come on woman you can do it." My voice hung in the centre of the cavernous room, then dropped like a stone in the middle. Useless.

My brain also being useless, my eyelids drifted closed. They fluttered open then settled back into sleep mode. Permanently.

No. No. Stop panicking. I don't mean death. I mean for the night. I woke with a start in the morning. Hungry, thirsty and fervently wishing I'd phoned the boys in blue the night before. My civic duty didn't feel quite so important this morning. I felt like civically shoving it right up Lord Lamont's jacksie. Along with every drug in the castle. That would teach him to mess with a Claymore.

Due to the lack of ideas on how to escape, I went for the tried and true method.

"Help. Help. Anyone there?"

I might as well be in space for all the notice anyone took. Was anyone else in the castle? Perhaps they'd all gone off on their holibobs and left me to it. The thought of starving to death didn't appeal. I might be a skinny dancer but I did eat. Talking of dancing, this incarceration was doing nothing for my fitness. I threw off a few kicks just for the sake of it.

My mind turned to the penny dreadfuls. What would the pulp fiction PI's do? I had a sneaking suspicion every last one of them would have a knife posed about their person. They'd grab it with their teeth, cut the ropes and be home by lunch time. Having arrested everyone in the process. This did little to console me as I can barely cope with a butter knife, never mind anything more lethal. And it's illegal to carry a knife in Scotland. Yes. I know I'm a detective. A well behaved one. Besides my mother would kill me if I broke the law. I was more scared of her than of the police.

Lack of knife or not, I still had to attempt some sort of escape from my shackles. Quite how this could be achieved escaped me. I struggled like a Victorian heroine tied to the train tracks. Where was my moustachioed hero when I needed him? Struggle proved futile. It only tightened my bonds which rubbed and hurt like all get out. My arms stretched out beyond human capability, had passed the stage of pain and reached excruciating. I used every tiny iota of my ballet training to tense and relax the muscles. I also did instant meditation. This helped. Did I say I was hungry?

The door opened, and a doddery butler appeared. Carrying a tray, he could have been the Messiah. Hallelujah. Right behind him came Desperate Dave Stallins himself. Carrying a gun. The gun pointed at me. At least I knew what job he did now. Lord Lamont's henchman. He didn't find that career down the job centre.

Doddery put the tray down and untied me.
    "Move and you'll never dance again."
    I didn't like to tell the weasel my dancing days were over anyway. Still, I'm sure he was as useless at shooting as everything else. In an attempt to kneecap me he'd shoot me right between the eyes.
    Having a gun waving around tends to put one off their breakfast. I still ate it. Coffee and a roll with jam, it wasn't exactly gourmet. But it was food. By this point, I would have eaten it if it came from an animal. Some vegetarian I was turning out to be.

"You're not such a big shot now, Claymore. Got everything you deserve."
    "If you're up to your unmentionables in all this, why did you drag me into it?"
    "Never thought you'd get this far. The only PI in the nation who couldn't find her own backside with loo roll."

"Charming as ever, Dave. Your old Ma would be proud.'

He whacked me on the side of the head with the gun. High bed and short man, don't make for the perfect aim. I still saw stars. These clichés were beginning to annoy me. Really annoy. I kicked in the direction of his head. Missed by a whisker.

This resulted in him ordering dodder to tie both my hands and feet.

I was trussed up and left to my fate.

I swear the dear old faithful retainer winked before he turned. Was he coming on to me? No way, he had to be about a hundred and nine.

"Do you know your boyfriend's dead," I shouted after Dave's back.

He slammed the door behind him.

Then I felt remorse. What a horrible thing to say. I really was making a right show of my mother.

Something else struck me. I should've asked to go to the loo before Dave and Dodder retired. I just knew I would regret drinking that coffee.

64

This left me wondering how I'd ever escape.

My thoughts drifted to Lady Lucy's role in this. Was she caught up in the shenanigans and I merely being used as a stool pigeon? If that was the right phrase. Who the heck knew.

I wished I'd read my PI correspondence course more closely. I'm sure there must be a section on extracting oneself from tight situations. Or one about not diving head first into tight situations in the first place. Fat lot of good it was right now.

I wriggled, lay still, shut my eyes, opened them, wriggled some more. This was excruciating. Boring didn't even begin to cover it.

To pass the time I thought about how Florian might have shuffled off this mortal coil. I would hazard a guess as to drugs. This brilliant deduction came about from the fact he didn't have a mark on him when he dropped at my feet. Apart from the bruise that came about via my own fair hands.

I wasn't too bothered about Roderic killing me. I reckon he'd have done it by now if he'd been serious about his intent. Feeding me implied he wanted me alive for something.

The butler's lack of surprise at my incarceration told me this was a regular occurrence in the Lamont household.

To pass the time I had another little nap. Dodder the

butler had left the bonds slightly looser so there was a little give and take. Now I knew what the wink indicated. Lovely man. I might just propose to him.

I was working on removing my bonds when I heard an almighty rumpus. Even the thick walls of the castle struggled to dull the sound. It included a lot of barking that sounded just like my dumb mutt. It couldn't be. Probably some Irish wolfhound or another hunting dog.

Before another thought could take up residence in my brain, the door crashed open and Eagal flew through it like the hounds of hell were after him.

My flabber couldn't be more gasted if it tried.

65

Who'd have thought Eagal's penchant for breaking down doors would save the day?

He lolloped over to me leapt on the bed and greeted me like a long-lost relative. By my reckoning I'd only been here about twenty-four hours, so his greeting was a tad effusive. His licking enthusiastic and thorough, it would save me having a shower. Or send me straight to the shower when I returned to the fold.

For once I didn't care. I let him do whatever he wanted, the wee hero.

Quill climbed up on the bed and untied me, so I hugged him. Then I hugged the dog. I drew the line at hugging the police officers who were milling around.

Lachie hugged me, and his mates cheered. I shoved him off. "Leave me alone, you daft bat. I'm fine, and you're on duty."

Freedom brought its own problems. Blood rushed to my extremities causing pain enough for two. I leapt around like a toddler learning a pas de chat. Wrist rubbing accompanied the steps.

"It would appear that you need myself and your canine companion to extricate you from your difficulties. Maybe having an assistant is exactly what you need."

Quill winked. That, his twinkling eyes and dapper appearance, gave him an insouciant charming look. There were times when I could see why all the women fell for those charms. This was one of them. If I wasn't already spoken for I'd be proposing to him.

Talking of being spoken for, Larbert dashed through the door accompanied by seven firefighters and a brace of paramedics. He and the paramedics fought to get near me. More hugging ensued. Then he kissed me in the way that staked his claim.

"Put her down, Mate. Let the green and yellow brigade do their stuff."

Lachie's voice, stern with a hint of laughter had the right effect. Larbert handed me over.

"Is there anyone left in the emergency services, or are you all here for the party?" I looked around. "Who called all you lot anyway? It's way OTT."

"I did, dear lady. I wasn't sure who would be required in the rescue effort, so I invited them all."

"What did you bring the shaggy rug..." I turned as a flash caught my eye. "Eagal, no."

The daft dog towards Lady Lucy who happened to be carrying little Theo. Fenella trailed behind her. Eagal taking out the entire Lamont family in one fell swoop would not do a lot for my reputation as a PI

With regards to the PI gig I had to get to the bottom of a few things.

"Did you know there are three rooms being used to store illegal substances in this castle."

"Way in front of you," said Lachie.

"I took the liberty of informing them of this useful fact. It aided in their arriving here with undue haste." The excitement of the occasion hadn't dulled my assistant's eloquence.

"What?" said Lady Lucy, "Where?" Her implacable face gave me the distinct impression she wasn't as surprised as her words might suggest.

"Where's Lord Lamont?"

Lachie tutted. "You ask too many questions."

"Stow it Lachie." My fiest had returned. "It's my case."

"Tucked up wearing handcuffs in a state-of-the-art police car."

"You need to find Dave Stallins as well." I rattled off what he'd done.

Lachie barked a few orders and several police officers scurried off.

Mrs McLellan would have a girly fit.

A couple of hours later most people departed, although the place was still crawling with coppers sorting out the drugs.

I stayed behind to talk to Lady Lamont.

"What are you going to do now?" I couldn't imagine her without all the trappings.

"What do you mean?"

"You'll lose your home."

Lucinda burst out laughing. "Cass, the castle and the money are in my name."

I gawped. Yes. Really.

"It was done years ago as a tax dodge. To answer your question. What I am going to do is enjoy my life and my children."

She bent down and pulled her cheque book and the Onoto fountain pen from her handbag.

"The first thing I am going to do is give you a huge bonus."

It was then *I* knew I was also going to enjoy my new life.

The End

Also by Wendy H Jones

THE DI SHONA McKENZIE MYSTERIES

Killer's Countdown
Killer's Craft
Killer's Cross
Killer's Cut
Killer's Crew
Killer's Crypt

FERGUS AND FLORA MYSTERIES

The Dagger's Curse
The Haunted Broch (Coming September 2018)

BERTIE THE BUFFALO (Picture Books)

Bertie's Great Escape (Coming October 2018)

FIND OUT MORE

Website: http://www.wendyhjones.com

WENDY H JONES

Wendy H. Jones lives in Dundee, Scotland, and Scottish Crime Books are set in the city.

Wendy, who is a committed Christian, has led a varied and adventurous life. Her love for adventure led to her joining the Royal Navy to undertake nurse training. After six years in the Navy she joined the Army where she served as an officer for a further 17 years. This took her all over the world including the Middle East and the Far East. Much of her spare time is now spent travelling around the UK, and lands much further afield.

As well as nursing Wendy also worked for many years in Academia. This led to publication in academic textbooks and journals.

Made in the USA
Middletown, DE
22 July 2022